To Bill : Joan —

PEOPLE
I
WANTED
TO BE

Blessings to you both!

BOOKS BY GINA OCHSNER

The Necessary Grace to Fall

People I Wanted to Be

GINA OCHSNER

PEOPLE
I
WANTED
TO BE

A Mariner Original
HOUGHTON MIFFLIN COMPANY
Boston / New York
2005

For information about permission to reproduce
selections from this book, write to Permissions,
Houghton Mifflin Company, 215 Park Avenue South,
New York, New York 10003.

Visit our Web site: www.houghtonmifflinbooks.com.

Library of Congress Cataloging-in-Publication Data
Ochsner, Gina, date.
People I wanted to be / Gina Ochsner.
p.   cm.
"A Mariner original."
ISBN 0-618-56372-5
I. Title.
PS3615.C48P46 2005
813'.6—dc22   2004065132

Book design by Melissa Lotfy

Printed in the United States of America

MP 10 9 8 7 6 5 4 3 2 1

The author is grateful to the editors of the following peri-
odicals, in which these stories first appeared: Carve, "From
the Fourth Row"; Fiddlehead, "When the Dark Is Light
Enough"; Image, "Signs and Markings"; Kenyon Review, "Ar-
ticles of Faith"; Mid-American Review, "Last Words of the
Mynah Bird"; The New Yorker, "The Fractious South";
Prairie Schooner, "A Blessing" (copyright © 1999 by the University of Nebraska Press); Turnrow, "How One Carries Another"; Whiskey Island Review and New Millennium Writing,
"The Hurler"; Words & Images, "Halves of a Whole."

"Darkness #11," by David Barker, is from Quartet (Bottle of Smoke Press, December 2003). Used by permission of
Bottle of Smoke Press.

This book is for Brian, Natasha, Soren, Connor, and Korey.
You are all walking, living evidence of the miraculous,
and each of you has made all the difference.

according to quantum physics
everything not forbidden can
and will happen.   that's both
very good and very bad news.

—DAVID BARKER,
"Darkness #11"

Contents

IN MEMORIAM,

for

LAUREL LEE THALER,

whose encouragement and example blessed so many

PEOPLE
I
WANTED
TO BE

Articles of Faith

THE GHOSTS of the three children set up residence in the kataa next to the fishing rods and burlap sacks of potatoes, behind the shovels and rakes. "Not kataa," Irina corrected Evin when he tried to describe the footprints in the sod. "And not sarai," she said, broadening her stance and placing her hands on her hips. "Shed." They were working on learning proper English, teaching their ears the subtleties of intonation, pitch, and diction. Though they lived in Karelia, which was shared by Finns and Russians, they had agreed he would drop his Finnish and she her Russian so they could carry a new language between them. But that had been when they were first married, nearly ten years ago, and now it seemed to Evin that English was simply one more language with which to misunderstand each other. And when they wanted to nettle each other, he'd noticed, they would retreat to their more familiar languages.

Last night they had listened to the shattering of glass. All night long they lay beneath their covers, guessing: bottles, or jars of the winter pears in heavy syrup she'd made the year before; *kholodets,* the meat in aspic, she guessed in Russian. A souvenir rifle, Evin's metal reel casing, his tackle box, he offered in Finnish. Finally they kicked off the covers, dressed in their thermals and boots, grabbed the flashlight, and went out to the sarai. The latch, a red-and-white fishing wire looped in a knot, had come unhooked, and the door wagged open and closed. Inside, puddles of broth and brine had begun to freeze at the edges.

"Maybe it was the neighbor boy," Irina said, and went to find a broom. Evin considered the boy from the other side of the laurel hedge — motherless and hollow-eyed, with a tendency to skulk — and shook his head. Through the window he saw movement in the pear tree just behind the shed. It was the ghosts, he decided, their ghost children, climbing the tree limbs and watching them mop up the shed. When he felt a prickling sensation, the hairs lifting along his forearms, he knew they'd come into the shed, passing themselves off, as they always did, as sudden shocks of chilly updrafts or, if it was daytime, as shafts of light, motes of dust, scraps of sky.

As he bent for a broken bottle, the neck a jagged collar of teeth, he could feel quick pushes of air around his elbow and the backs of his knees. Last week, while picking stones out of the little potato field, he had felt them behind him, and all the rest of that day Evin had kept jerking his arm, throwing out the point of his elbow to see if he could catch them unawares, maybe finally glimpse them. Now, as he reached for a bucket for the shards, a draft lifted the hair off his forehead.

On her papers Irina was listed as Karel, and therefore a Finn. But her mother had been Russian and Irina had received a Soviet education. By the time she met Evin, she had forgotten what little Finnish she had once known and preferred to think in Russian, pray in Russian, and shout in Russian. Russian was a roomier language, and what was language anyway but vague ideas looking for clothes to wear?

"English," the matchmaker who lived near the lumberyard had insisted. All the offices in the yards were adopting the English-only rule, and Irina had better learn it if she wanted to work her way into the lumber office, especially if she wanted to find a hardworking and sober man who'd strayed across the Finnish-Karelian border.

And so they lied—a small lie. Vaina, the matchmaker, told Evin Haanstra, a thirty-eight-year-old bachelor, that Irina had passed second-year English courses with a troika. "A three—nothing to sneeze at!" Vaina told Evin more than once. Evin shrugged. For him, speaking English was like stomping around barefoot in the dark. But if Irina wanted to speak English, fine, and if it convinced Aila, her supervisor at the lumber office, to give her a promotion, that was fine too. He wanted a Russian girl, that much he knew. The Finnish girls never even gave him a nod, and he liked the way Karelian girls knew how to wear makeup and even flirt a little. And so he paid Vaina what she asked, a month's wages. She pulled out a work pencil, one of the thick square ones used in the yard, and licked the nib.

"You have a rare soul," Evin said in Finnish, and Vaina, seated behind her blocky desk in the corner of the office, translated the message to Irina. The translation was not the best—*Let's have radishes in the shower*—but the match went through anyway. Irina stitched the family icons of Saint Seraphim, Saint Boris, and Saint Gleb, and of course the Theotokos, Mother of God, to the stays of her wedding dress, and in the end everyone agreed that it was a good match, all things considered. Evin had provided everything he had promised: a small house outside Petrozavodsk with a plot for potatoes and even a shed that doubled as a coop for her geese. The only thing he hadn't been able to give her was living, breathing children. And for this, he knew, Irina harbored a small cache of anger.

Irina withdrew her little calendar from the kitchen drawer and circled the numbers of the days she was fertile. On the days circled in red, she pulled the calendar back out at night and drew an X at the bottom of the square, after she and Evin tried to make a child. Now she flipped through the calendar and sighed. All those X's and still no children. All those months, each one passed as another exercise in grief.

Irina snapped off the light and squeezed her eyes shut. Evin was still out in the shed sweeping up that mess, while all around her, in houses in other fields, couples were making love, making babies without worry or even much effort. It made her sick. People who didn't care either way would finish their business and drop off to sleep, some of them pregnant already. Irina considered her supervisor at the yard office. Aila had once confided to Irina that she had a deep and abiding fear that she would make a bad mother and that she had never wanted children. Now Aila had a little girl, and her biggest concern was how to get rid of the weight she'd gained from the pregnancy.

Anger bloomed in Irina's chest, the muscles along her jaw tightening. A bad joke, this life. She'd always believed hard work brought you what you wanted. That's what she'd been taught, that's what she had come to expect. In Karelia, a divided land of upland and rock, water and forest, the soil would give if you just worked hard enough. Irina sighed. Now the hardest work Aila did was to sit behind her particleboard desk and clench her butt muscles when she thought no one was looking. But the way her face gripped at her mouth as if she'd heard a dirty story and was trying hard not to laugh made it obvious to Irina.

Evin had first noticed the children a few months ago, on his way out to the sarai to check his fish drying on the racks. He loved his shed, a rundown shack of peeling tarpaper and shingles. He loved the smell of the fresh sawdust Irina spread over the floor, the drying rowan and cowberries hanging in swatches. He loved the diesel fumes and the oil that beaded up as a dark resin along the old boards on hot days. He even loved the smell of the lake salmon and the scent of the mud from the lakes on the tips of his fingers. He was thinking of all this when he opened the door and instantly smelled something new: a clean, brisk aroma, like the rush of air from a freezer when the door is yanked wide.

Then he observed the rattling of his rods, the tarpaper peeling from the boards. At the same moment he felt a shift in the air, and he knew that whatever it was had passed by and gone outside. Evin followed it, stood next to the birch tree, and pointed his nose north, toward the swamp. The air was still, as if it were holding its breath. Evin thought he could just see the outlines of three children as they jostled one another and kicked their feet in the tree. He stood without moving for a moment, then jumped, reaching for their ankles.

It must have been the cold, Irina had said matter-of-factly, her eyes flat and gray. Evin had stumbled into the kataa, breathless, anxious to tell her what he'd seen. Irina had just driven the geese through the yard and into the small pens Evin had built for them, and she was now killing and dressing them, one by one. "Those couldn't have been our children out in the tree." She clapped a goose between her legs, pulled its neck alongside its back, and gave a hard twist, falling backward on her heels.

"It could be the cold," Evin agreed in Finnish. They both knew that the cold could make you clumsy, make you silly, wishing for the impossible. The lowering frost could make you see things, make you parse figures from the shadows.

But that night he heard the back door rattle open and shut as gusts of wind plied it. Later he heard laughter, a liquid sound like water bubbling over, and then, near daybreak, a bumping around the hearth and a *whoosh, whoosh,* as if they were taking turns sliding down the flue.

. . .

Up there in the birch, a sickly thing that Evin had promised Irina he'd chop down. Sometimes in the shed. Of course she knew the children were there. She wasn't blind. She saw how the wind riffled the blackened leaves, how it missed certain patches, those dips and grooves in the limbs, the best spots for sitting. On still days she'd seen a wiggle in the topmost branch. Twice she'd heard the shout of laughter, once a tiny, gasping cry. Now that the frost had set as a sheer veil over the field, she sometimes heard their little feet scraping over the ground. She would have loved to gather them into her arms, bury her nose in the napes of their necks, taking in their warm, oily smell. She would have loved to run her fingers over theirs, cup her palm around their heels, or count their toes. She would have done all these things and more, but they were not real, she knew. Real enough to displace air, but not real enough to hold, to kiss, to rock.

Perhaps she had not given them enough attention during their earliest days, and perhaps that was why they were here now, trying to be noticed. While they were in the womb, as sinew was meshing with the soft, trellislike bones, there must have been too many moments when she was thinking of other things—her geese, Evin's fish, the lumberyard. Perhaps she didn't pray steadily enough. Perhaps she and Evin were speaking their separate languages and there was a pause, a word dropped, and that was the moment when the babies were lost, when their tiny hearts grew weak, stopped fluttering, and she didn't even know it.

All summer long and into the fall, a short season marked only by a change in the wind's strength and direction, she knitted sweaters and mittens and thigh-high socks for them. But they weren't cold, she finally decided. If they were, they'd curl up in front of the fire she fed every night until looking at the flames began to pull her toward sleep. They weren't cold, just curious. She could feel their little eyes drinking in every detail of color and substance, every movement, so that later at night they would have something to dream about. She hoped they weren't watching and listening to everything she said and did. The English she used around the house—it wasn't so good. And while she never used to bother with matters of modesty, she'd recently taken to shutting and even locking the door to the toilet.

She hoped they were not huddling under the bed or hiding in the closet on the days circled in red. At the ends of these days, she put away her knitting early and she and Evin went to bed. She would pull up her nightgown to her navel, the signal for Evin to unbuckle his trousers. Even with her eyes squeezed shut as she prayed earnestly for conception, for the perfect forming of fingers and eyelashes, elbows and roots of teeth, an uneasy feeling would wash over her. It was a creepy feeling the Karelians described as *jaa ssa veri,* to be living among the dead, seen by the unseen—an expression having to do with ice in the blood.

Afterward, Irina would pull her nightgown back over her hips and straighten it around her knees. Evin would kiss her quickly on the forehead, for luck, and then thump down the stairs and out the back door to the shed, where, she knew, he'd rearrange his spinners and lures. She would lie perfectly still, her whole body tightened into a hard fist as she listened to the dogs barking. From that moment forward, her every thought would be fixed on keeping what was inside her from spilling back out. She even followed Aila's lead, clenching the muscles of her butt into fierce knots, as well as that female muscle Vaina had told her about with a wink. Irina practiced squeezing that one too, while she lay flat on her back.

At last, when she thought that whatever was supposed to happen had had long enough either to do it or not, she would kick her legs out from under the covers. She'd rise from the bed and kneel in front of the icon of the Theotokos, a raised metal image of Mary holding little baby Jesus. It was difficult, looking at Mary. Irina would feel that familiar anger, faithful and unbidden, like a dog at her heels. Here was one more mother who hadn't even tried. But then Irina would make the sign of the cross and bend to kiss the little Jesus. This was when she'd feel the children drawing near, and she could sense that they were sad. "I'm sorry," she would have liked to tell them, for she was sure that she was to blame in some way. Then she would climb back into bed, a shiver taking hold in her spine, her hands clammy. She'd hold her breath, waiting for the children to go back out to the shed.

During the six months the children had lived in the yard, Evin had noticed that they preferred to play in the kataa. Maybe because it was where Irina kept the geese, and, longing to see more of their mother, they curled themselves around Irina's many hooks and knives as well as his tools, his rods and reels. That was the only way he could explain it, why they would prefer the cold, the cracking frost that pinched the nose and eyebrows and squeezed down on the ribs. Still, it bothered him that they were out there, and every night for the past week, after Irina drifted to sleep, Evin had crept from his bed, heated up mugs of hot chocolate, and set them along the windowsill of the shed.

For the children were astonishingly normal in some ways. They liked the hot chocolate he brought. They also liked to play games and practical jokes. One of them—or maybe they were taking turns—moved Evin's eyeglasses so that when he woke in the morning, all he could see was a watery world of light and shadow. This morning he was on his hands and knees, feeling around for the frames. Just when his fingers brushed the rims, he felt a small current of air and his glasses skittered out of reach. Evin laughed, sitting back on his haunches in surrender. He remembered being a boy, teasing his father in the small ways children do.

"Pull!" A fierce shout rose now from behind the laurel hedge, and Evin jumped to his feet. The neighbors, the father and his seven-year-old son, were out in the yard. Evin could hear the man teaching the boy to shoot at clay pigeons, only they didn't have a launcher, so the father was standing behind a pile of stones and lobbing up a clay disk. They didn't have a rifle either, so the boy threw a rock at the clay pigeon as it plummeted back to the ground. The man was teaching his son the importance of aim, of watchfulness. But the boy was a bad shot, and Evin could see how this frustrated the father, made him wring his hands.

From behind the bedroom window, Evin watched another disk climb the air slowly, then fall gracelessly, the air being too thin for such birds without wings. The exercise seemed absurd to him. Evin recalled his lovemaking sessions with Irina: they were grim affairs, lacking joy, which, he had discovered, was not the same as passion, which they also lacked. Over time these sessions had begun to feel like a chore, what people did to prove to themselves they still felt and behaved the way married people should. But what went wrong, he asked aloud, when these children, these shapes now sliding across the floor, were sorting themselves into being deep inside Irina's belly?

Evin spread his fingers over the glass pane and watched the man with his boy.

"Now!" the father shouted, and the boy cocked his arm and launched a rock. Evin saw the rock skate past the disk.

Maybe Evin loved fishing too much. Maybe, his mind spinning with floats, flies, reels, and bait, he hadn't wanted a baby badly enough. Maybe he'd wanted one for all the wrong reasons. "Live," he had prayed the last time that Irina had had contractions and begun to bleed. "Too soon," she had gasped, and he had realized he wanted that baby to live so Irina could finally have the child she so longed for. He had wanted her to have that child so she would finally be happy. So full with love for a child, he imagined her heart would spill over with extra affection, enough even for him.

Evin rocked forward, leaned his weight on his palms. A timid snow was falling. It wouldn't last long, but the boy was excited anyway, sticking his tongue out in joy.

"Watch now! You're not watching!" Evin could hear how the father's frustration had tipped to anger. Maybe after the thaw Evin could ask the boy if he'd like to go fishing with him. He'd seen the way the boy watched him as he worked the hoe, seen how his eyes, hungry for the sight of a woman, followed Irina when she was in the yard with the geese. Those were the moments when Evin permitted himself to imagine that this boy was his son.

"Oh, forget about it!" The father threw up his hands in defeat. Evin stepped back from the window. He slid the glasses from the perch on his nose and set them on the table, so that later the children would have something to play with.

She loved the children in the shed. She just wished they would take what they'd come back for, whatever that was—her affection, her blessings—take it and go away, leave them alone. Irina stepped cautiously out into the snow, holding a steaming pan of bread wrapped in a towel. They would be five and three and two years old by now. They'd have questions and might want answers. Well, what was she supposed to say? Something in her made her want children, she could not help that. And something in her wouldn't let her have them. For some reason her body spun children with flawed architecture. Irina stepped through the crust of ice over the yard. With the first one, the end had happened so early in the pregnancy that she could have fooled herself into thinking she'd never been pregnant at all. But with the second she had felt her body changing, the blood throbbing behind her fingernails and in her gums, a swell in her stomach. Just before she miscarried there had been movement. Then nothing but heavy stillness. When she thought of that one, she imagined a cup of milk going sour, curdling and flaking to paste. The last one she doesn't allow herself to think about.

She unhooked the fishing wire, pushed open the door, and waited a moment for the geese to scatter. She withdrew a handkerchief from her pocket and brushed some sod and feathers from the top of a crate. Then she set the bread down. Careful to keep her eyes from the top shelves of the shed and from the limbs of the tree, she turned for the house. Still, she could feel their little eyes fastened on her as she passed by the birch. Irina stopped short at the foot of the tree and counted the last of the leaves. She closed her eyes and imagined a baby tucked in the hollow between her neck and her shoulder. She pictured the tiny fingers that would curl around her own, the feet like the petals of a rose. And the soles! Irina paused to rub her forefinger and thumb together. Soles with the softness of skin that has never touched the ground.

How she longed to have the faith, the imagination, to believe that it was still possible. Then it might not be so hard. She might not hate other mothers so much, might not resent Aila for giving her grief about her hours. The time off hadn't been her fault, she told the children in the tree. Not her fault that she'd been calling in sick so often. Who wouldn't feel sick — sick in the heart, in the spirit?

And angry too. Irina scowled. *"Proch otsyda!"* Scat! She waved her hands as if trying to frighten crows from a perch.

"We did what we could! What else is there?" She shook her skirt at the tree. Then she pulled a sharp breath through her teeth and held it. She heard a furtive rustling in the hedge and the crack of frozen leaves. They were leaving. Irina turned on her heel, then bit her lip so hard she drew blood, for she spied the neighbor boy behind her, retreating through the frozen stand of laurel.

He went less for the pike and perch than for the stillness of the water and the quiet. But for all the water, there were never enough fish. To go to Ladoga, though, or even Onega, to inhale the sweet dampness that hung like a cloud over the dark water, was a kind of healing.

He went there to get away from Irina. She had developed the habit of having too many habits. For example, pressing her mouth into a frown. He'd once loved the way she didn't need a reason to laugh, the way her laughter erupted from her and could fill an entire room. And her stomach, flat and hard like the back of a shovel's head. But since they'd married he had witnessed her slowly turning quiet and cross, packing herself full of blintzes and sweets. Now her stomach had gotten spongy.

Evin brought the hoe down hard into the soil. Hope only filled you with expectation. At night Irina buried her face in her pillow and cried. In the morning he'd rise early, go to the lake, and make it his home for a day. He'd tuck the reel between his elbow and his side and watch for the possibility of grace, a bit of heavenly kindness dropped here on the flat surface of the water, shown there in the fierce span of an eagle's wings here in his tired heart, which still managed to want what it wanted.

Evin stopped and leaned against the hoe. He was talking to the tree now, but so what. All this waiting for a group of cells to divide without any help from him. All this believing that someday he would have something he could hold in his arms, a proof of his love, something that he could spend the rest of his life showing his love to—all this had worn him down.

Evin craned his neck. Something on the top branch wiggled, and a small flurry of leaves drifted onto his head and shoulders, then piled at his feet. He heard a whimper and, a few seconds later, a sneeze so close to his ear it raised the hairs on the back of his neck. Then the deliberate crack of a branch, a fluttering from the laurel hedge, a pair of small white hands.

"Wait!" Evin called out.

It was nearing Christmas. Though it was only three in the afternoon, the sun had blanched to a faint and fading light. The freeze was so deep that the trucks and haul lines in the yards ran twenty-four hours a day to save the engines. The pike and perch were frozen solid in the lakes, and it was time for all things dying to be done. This was what Evin was thinking one afternoon when he climbed the stairs to the bedroom and nudged Irina's elbow. "I'm going to cut down that tree now," he said.

"Then cut it," Irina snapped. She pulled the covers over her head and burrowed deep into the bed, where she'd been for the past three days.

Evin trudged down the stairs and out through the yard. Nothing seemed to know its end until it was too late. He recalled the quickness of his wife's hands, how they did not falter, how her geese never had a chance to honk. And now here they were in the shed, hung up for winter, thick in their shells of ice.

He moved his tackle box, rearranged his rods. Finally he grabbed the ax and went to stand under the tree. He studied the splay of limbs and how they separated the sky into bolts of color that were quickly dissolving into night, first in swatches of rose, then lavender, then ashy blue. Each of the last leaves stood out sharp and true above the children dodging and darting around one another. Evin put his hands on his hips. There was something important he wanted to ask. *What was it?* he thought, but his lips formed the word *Why?*

Behind the hedgerow the neighbor had switched on his sulfur lights. The yellow-orange glow cut hazy circles in the lowering frost. Evin stood on tiptoe, squinting at the man and his boy, who were sitting on their back steps. The man was teaching his son how to weather the cold by stamping his feet and holding his breath. But even from this distance Evin could hear the boy's teeth chattering. The man began reciting philosophical axioms and then reading a fairy tale about cold and bundles of matches blooming like flowers of fire.

"Now just listen, listen to this," the man said as he read. He clasped his hands together at his chest for dramatic effect. "'Mother, I am coming!' the little match girl said, lighting match after match to preserve the image of her mother held in the halo of each flame." He unclasped his hands, licked the tip of his finger, and turned a page. The boy's jaw had locked, and his hands were cupped to his face.

Evin turned back to the tree. Whether or not he and Irina were granted their wish, whether they ever had real children or just these ghosts, he would have to learn to content himself with what he had. He would give in and believe that this kind of faith could satisfy him and these children here, slipping among the shadows, were tokens of such faith. He would continue going to the lakes, picking stones from his field, doing what he'd always done, because there was nothing else he could do. He stopped to consider the falling light. And then, because it felt good to be doing something rather than nothing, he cocked his arm and lobbed the ax as far as he could out into the frozen potato field, where he heard it land with a small thud. He stood on tiptoe to see if he could catch sight of the blade glinting, and turned for the shed.

Irina pulled on Evin's workboots but left the laces undone. A small stack of sweaters spilled over the wicker of her knitting basket and onto the floor. She gave the basket a nudge with a boot. Then she gathered the sweaters into her arms. They weren't finished. She hadn't set the shirring at the waist on the blue one, and the arms had come unraveled where the children had pulled at them. Still, Irina stumped down the stairs and closed the kitchen door behind her. Then she crossed the yard and stood under the tree, where the leaves had all fallen, bringing the sky back in view. The air had grown stern and piercing. She could hear Evin rattling around in the shed, and in the yard next to theirs she could hear *plink, plink, plink,* the sounds of the neighbor boy pitching flat rocks while his father read to him from an enormous book.

"I'm ready now," she said aloud, not caring who heard. She kneeled on the frozen ground and placed the tangle of sweaters at the foot of the tree. The children were not hers to have. Not these ghosts spiriting the house, haunting her dreams, even now kicking in the branches of this tree. Irina felt the cold in the ends of the boots.

"I'm sorry," she said at last, her hands hanging limply from her wrists. "I'm so sorry. We wanted you all very badly." She wiped at her nose. But it was time, she told them, pitching her voice to the lowest limb of the tree. Time to be at peace here with this tree, and with her body, though it pained her in a way she had never thought possible. She would throw away the calendar with all the ridiculous X's and say to herself in every language she knew and as many times as it took until she believed it that whatever was to be would be, what should happen would.

Irina stood on tiptoe and watched the boy next door throw rocks into the air. Perhaps she would be entrusted with someone else's child for a day or two. Or even just for an hour. And she would love that child as if it were hers, she would give it every good thing, bestow on it every good wish and intention. She would tell him how beautiful he was, perfect in design, how amazing the symmetry of soul and body. She would tell him how glad she was that even if her own children couldn't sit in her lap and listen as she told stories to the time of her clacking needles, this child could, and what a miracle, what an incredible miracle that was.

Irina tightened the knot in her scarf. She could sense them going quietly now, past the tree and through the short field to the laurels. They were leaving as suddenly as they had come, going back to the lakes, to the dark waters and the frozen marshes, going in a lighthearted flutter of frozen leaves. She tipped her head. Through the limbs of the trees, an early show of stars bloomed against the dark. She could read in the scattering a fist here, an ear curved and set against a round shoulder there. If she squinted she could force a rib to connect to a breastbone, a breastbone to the yoke of a shoulder, and squinting this way she imagined she could compose such children of the very heavens.

Evin pulled the shed door closed and rehooked the fishing wire. What sadness, for he had developed a fondness for, a familiarity with these ghost children, who so often reminded him of himself as a young boy. He would miss their pushes at the elbow, those cold pockets of air folding against his body.

Evin crossed the yard and stopped a few paces behind Irina, who stood with her hands resting on her hips, looking through the tree as far into the future as possible.

Last Words
of the Mynah Bird

I'M FAMOUS. You wouldn't think so to look at me, with my triple chins, double knees, and full apron of flesh hanging over my belt, all this and my terrible overbite as well. But it's true.

It seems strange, even to me, because all my thirty-eight years I was a nobody. Simply a nothing.

How things change, how the worm turns, my wife, Vitasha, would say, cutting herself another slice of cake. She's fat too, and we like it that way. Life hasn't been so good that we'd like to prolong it by following some ridiculous diet with the fervor of those who've found true religion. We see such people passing by our open windows in summer and fall, sprinting as if they're afraid they'll miss a bus. It's madness, and it hurts my knees to watch.

My biggest question now is how to tell my story. Pacing —and even direction—trouble me to no end. Forward or reverse? It would be easy if my life were a continuous episode, the neat threads of theme running warp and weft, fore and aft. Alas, nothing is so simple, not even for me. Sometimes I hear knocks at our door: the neighbors hunting for advice they think only a famous person will have. Only a blinkered mind seeks help from someone of my troubled celebrity, I tell them, gently closing the door. What I don't say is how my problems started only days after I brought home the mynah bird. Through the courtyard, past the statue of horses cast in mid-gallop, I carried the bird, my coat draped over his wire cage so the horses would not scare him—this bird, who, according to the pet-store owner, had an excitable nature.

It might have been better to mention the mynah bird straight off, to foreshadow and nudge at the proper hierarchy of things, but too few writers favor their audience with a genuine surprise. Though sometimes the story demands several tellings before a sense of proportion is reached by the teller, who discovers, to his astonishment, that the tale is not about his ever-widening girth, or even the fractious marriage that has been teetering along like a three-legged horse and that precipitated the purchase of the mynah bird.

Being married so many years, I love my wife terribly. That is to say, I love her best when we are apart. Shortly after we married, her true and quarrelsome nature revealed itself in the purchase of too many handbags and in her incessant nagging, which is like water drip-drip-dripping onto stone, dripping against my tender tympanic membrane. Not since our wedding day, when we said "I do" at the civil bureau, have we agreed on anything. Which begs the question, why did we marry? Because, as I explained to her many times while she pelted me with old handbags and battered copies of philosophy books, I had found her pretty. There you have it.

Certainly we sought help. I scoured the aisles of popular psychology books at the bookstore. Vitasha listened to call-in radio programs while eating small pastries with an alarming fastidiousness. Being unable to find a hobby besides our troubled marriage, and not wanting the noise and bustle of children, we took the advice of my doctor, the therapist, the bookstore owner, and the shopkeeper in the pet store. I roamed among the bright chatterings and belligerent squawks until I found the mynah bird. Stout and sturdy, with multiple wattles, he reminded me of myself. When he looked at me with his solemn amber eyes, I knew he was the one for us. With our attention focused on the bird, surely our marriage would be stronger. And so I brought the mynah bird home. To calm our tumultuous marriage. To restore sanity. To quiet the thunder that began each morning in the bedroom with careless words like "Stupid!" or "Fatty!" and brought all our neighbors to attention.

The bird was mute, as some mynahs are, waiting, we supposed, to hear the right words to unlock its tongue like a proper dose of crankcase oil. For days we studied him and ran our fingers along the length of his glossy black feathers. In the morning before I went to work, in the evening as the swifts bickered in the eaves, we got down on our hands and knees beside the cage to cluck, coo, and whistle. But day after day the bird sat there, staring back at us silently. In the mornings we began sharing our chocolate cake with him. We reminded ourselves that bears can be taught to dance in the moonlight to complicated waltzes and mazurkas. Patience, we breathed.

To be honest, I liked the bird's taciturn nature. While my wife quarreled endlessly over this and that ("When will you be promoted?" "When will we have a decent holiday?"), Tima — for such a quiet name seemed right for such a demure bird — merely listened with a calmness that astonished me. And he was an excellent arbiter. After my wife had spent her rage, had dashed the most precious of her family heirlooms against the porcelain of the kitchen sink, I'd plead my case to him, divining from the empty return of his amber eyes that he sided with me.

"Tima, do you hear that? Do you hear how the stupid cow

abuses me?" I'd cry, throwing my hands in the air. After I left the room, I'd hear my wife asking similar questions of him. Still he maintained an impassive silence.

But after a while his eerie quiet began to wear on us. We fought, I suspected, just to make noise, and our arguing rang empty in our own ears. We longed to hear the noise of a bird singing the vowels of our empty language, and if not that, then just the ordinary clicks and whistles of a pet in a cage.

Pepperoni sausage, the hottest I could find, was what finally did it. Cruel, some might say. But I had run out of ideas, and we needed the mitigating noise of the mynah bird. The pet-store owner assured me that spicy meats would make almost any animal break out in song, and I had turned desperate.

One blue-gray morning, just after Vitasha smashed a Sèvres teacup against the sink, Tima spoke.

"Shut your cake hole," he said in a strange and atonal voice as he bobbed his head and tucked his beak under a wing. Odd, I thought, for those were the very words I had said to Vitasha the other morning. And odd, that of all the things I had said to her that day, these were the words the bird remembered, these the words he chose to repeat.

"What was that you just said to me?" Vitasha turned from the sink, an expensive teapot raised dangerously above her head.

"Not me, darling, the bird," I said, winking in Tima's direction.

"That's right, imbecile," he called out—to whom, I wasn't sure.

From that day forward we could not get Tima to shut up. We draped a sheet over his cage, as a magazine suggested. We turned down the lights. We played soothing orchestral music. And still Tima babbled all day long and during the night in a barrage of clicks, warbles, and squeaks. It occurred to us that he might be singing. Only his murmuring included clips and phrases of the worst words Vitasha and I used. We listened in horror as he repeated, with an accuracy that astounded us, our vitriolic language.

The apartment swelled with Tima's shrill noise, his curses and invectives, Vitasha's hard replies, and my own occasional barks. Lovely, I thought, waltzing around in my underwear. We had foisted on this bird our incredible lacks and faults of character. The insults and complaints we normally saved for each other we now hurled at the bird.

But news of our bird's talents soon leaked out. Before we knew it, the neighbors started popping in at all hours to hear what Tima was saying. Sometimes it was a fortune cookie prediction, other times the formula for a time machine or a recitation of the eight proven steps to anger management. It turned out Tima had a knack for repeating gospel songs, the kind that must be carried off in a series of shrieks. Certainly he did his best. Listening to him inspired artistic notions of my own. Alongside the local newspaper clips of Tima that I collected in a notebook, I began writing down everything the bird said and to whom.

In the way that spectacle begets more spectacle, we were soon besieged by more curious, bored people. The oily pop of flashbulbs, the bustle of newspaper reporters in the corridor — it all began to make my arteries feel crowded. I thought Tima might notice my distress. I hoped he might let up. But did he? No, not for a minute. In fact, he seemed even more loquacious than before, prattling against purpose. What was worse, his words had grown quite indignant.

"What is the meaning of this?" he demanded when the frail old man from down the hall waved his useless but still shiny war medal at him. "How dare you afflict me thus!" Tima shouted in his flat and uninflected voice, to the great delight of the neighbors.

But in the calm moments before neighbors had yet arrived or when they had just left, Tima turned his attention to my wife and me, passing judgment in his nasal voice, repeating the words he'd heard us scream at each other as he proclaimed us tyrants and victims of our own villainy, the kind of wretches who could hate a saint—and without provocation, too. "How can you live?" he squawked with each chime of my wife's enormous grandfather clock.

Having never mastered halftones and having apparently forgotten the redemptive power of silence, Tima and his wretched voice began to hurt my ears. I marveled at the hard chatter issuing from the craw and beak of such a small creature. I wondered at the sheer volume and solemnity of it all. In all of this, I couldn't help observing that Tima had a serious shortcoming: he had absolutely no sense of humor and was altogether lacking in the gaiety one normally associates with birds of the starling family.

"Why shouldn't he be glum? You burned his tongue with sausage!" Vitasha said one night.

"Yes, it's true and I've admitted it already, but his dour nature points to something deeper in his essential character, don't you think?" I asked her.

Vitasha rolled onto her side and merrily dozed off. While she slept, Tima's interrogation continued. "Who? What? Why?" Tima squawked consistently and savagely. At last, in the early morning, when the liquid ticks of the clock sang behind my inner ear, Tima quieted down. The garbage trucks rumbled outside the window, and I heard Tima rustling his feathers in a tremulous fluttering.

"I have a desire to know God," his thin voice finally warbled in the predawn darkness. Then I heard excrement dropping onto the bottom of his cage.

I blame Kierkegaard entirely for what happened next, for

when I heard Tima's supplication, I heaved myself out of bed and lined the inside of his cage with my extra copies of the man's philosophy texts. That kept him quiet for a few hours. But by morning Tima, apparently a great reader, began spouting spiritual insights and pithy observations.

"Purity of heart is to will one thing," his voice warbled.

"Don't kid yourself," I returned, bringing my finger to the cage and tapping the bar. Tima took my finger in his curved beak. Then he bit it. Hard.

That was around the time I began grinding my teeth at night, and Vitasha claimed I began shouting in my sleep, "Silence, for God's sake!" And at other times, "Have mercy!"

Despite my nocturnal unrest, Tima seemed in better spirits. In the mornings Vitasha ignored my jokes but laughed at Tima's humorless retellings of them. So on it went for a few days, I leaving for work worn down by Tima's abuse, and Vitasha, in her organza nightgown, a pastry in hand, being entertained by the bird while our apartment slowly filled with guests.

And then the impossible happened. On a Saturday, a beautiful, languid Saturday, a day for oranges and coffee, chocolates and orchestral music, I went out to buy us a new set of teacups. When I returned, I discovered Vitasha wearing a lurid red negligee I'd never seen before and Tima perched on her shoulder. Tima, who had so faithfully repeated my every utterance, said into Vitasha's ear, "I love you," with a quiet, nasal twang. There was no mistaking what I heard. These were words I had never spoken to my wife, not in the presence of the bird, not before I'd purchased the bird.

"Curses!" I shouted, overcome with pure hatred. "You ingrate! You swine!" I shouted at Tima. "After all I've done for you!" I stamped my feet, and Vitasha burst into tears.

"How dare you!" she cried.

"How dare you!" Tima repeated, lifting from his perch on Vitasha's shoulder and resettling inside his open cage.

"I take back all my kisses!" Vitasha fled from the room in a torrential flood of tears and cursing.

I drew up a chair and sat opposite Tima. I sat like this until dusk fell, studying him as he sat, as quiet as a church mouse in his cage.

"I said nothing about silence," Tima said at last. "I said nothing about love."

Since human mercy is weak and memory faulty, I found it necessary to write unceasingly and in great detail the events of these past days, before the truth changed its shape on the cracked and blistered tongue of our mynah bird. Tima assured me regularly that his words to Vitasha meant nothing, had been merely a joke. But when I looked at him in disbelief, he showered me with a torrent of abusive words about man, God, saints, and beasts.

I would have done anything to shut him up. Anything to return him to his previous calm and mute state, anything not to hear what he had to say. With utter detachment, he repeated all that I had forgotten or could not bear to hear. With each squawk, Tima chipped away at the truth ("Lo, I am a prophet! He who has ears!") of what kind of man ("wretched sloth!") I was, revealing the darkness I thought I had so expertly hidden from myself ("selfish!"), revealing it as a goat licking salt lays bare the rocks of the earth.

For a week Vitasha and I avoided each other. She wanted neither to see me nor to touch me, nor to suffer to think about the same things I was considering. I had no idea what was going through her head, though we sat at the same table, slept in the same bed, and passed each other in the hallway—without speaking, of course, never speaking.

With no one to talk to, I whispered quietly to myself in the mirror, careful to keep my voice at a low and even pitch in fear of what Tima might hear and later repeat.

A week went by. Then two. Vitasha gained weight with a vengeance and wouldn't even glance at me. She wasn't looking at the bird either, and this gave me reason to hope.

"I'm sorry," I said to her at last. I'd just come in from the rain, in my hands a salted eel I'd brought back from the shop.

"I'm sorry too," she said with a colossal sniff.

"It's the damned bird," I said, rage toward Tima rising up within me.

"Yes, I suppose it is," Vitasha said quietly.

My hatred for Tima, while undiluted, was divided. I was angry at this bird, this bird who was supposed to save our marriage, and angry ("stupid!") at myself for believing it could. That night we lay awake in bed, studying our respective spheres of the ceiling, while Tima spoke as if gravel were stuck in his craw: "Love me, you ingrate! You swine!"

At four in the morning, the garbage trucks rumbled below our windows and Vitasha sighed.

"You can listen to only so much of him," I said, grinding my teeth.

"Certain words belong just to humans," she rejoined.

"Well said," I replied, thinking that these certain words could flute the edge of the tongue, slow the blood, settle the heart. Then I began to imagine Tima's softly feathered neck in the grip of my fingers, his craw pressed against my palm.

I secretly longed for an aircraft to drop on half the apartment and level Tima to a pulp. Yet never had Vitasha and I been so united, so harmonious in thought and action, as in this.

The next evening came in a hush of lamplight and condensation on the windowpanes. Vitasha conspicuously removed herself after dinner to the bathroom, where I could smell an overheated curling iron frizzing the air. Tima carried on as he always did after evening tea and brandy, a symphony with no nuance circling in his throat. He stopped midnote and called "Halt!" for now I was approaching.

Tima looked at me as if I were an utterly foreign being. "Please roll down your sleeves," he said. "You are frightening me."

"Prophets never make out well, for all the same reasons visionaries tend to go blind," I gently reminded him as I carried him, still in his cage, out of our apartment, down the corridor, down the stairs, through the courtyard, and to the back of the building.

"Don't!" he cried as I set the cage on a bench.

"Hush, now," I said, opening his cage door and prodding him out with a long stick I found on the ground. "Fly," I said. "Fly to other windows, plague other marriages. Speak in other tongues."

Tima hopped up and down the length of the bench. He flapped his wings once, twice, and then he was up and over the roofline. I left the open cage on the bench and walked to the courtyard, my hands shaking. The air was cooling, and I sat on the edge of the enormous fountain, the gilt-green horses covered in pigeon smear. In the murky water of the fountain, beneath the horses' enormous hooves, I studied the reflection of the dim stars. I sat like that for a good many minutes, asking myself what I had done, what Vitasha would think, knowing full well the answers.

At last I got up, walked through the courtyard, up the flights of stairs, and back into the apartment. Under the unfurling night sky, I told myself, the evening had suddenly grown a bit larger.

How One Carries Another

What I remember of St. Petersburg: being crammed inside an electric trolley, my nose buried in a man's armpit. Behind me, a woman carrying bags of books. Outside the fogged windowpanes of the trolley, we could see the bend in the tracks and around the bend, a stalled Niva. Electricity sparked in webs along the wire nets above the streets. From the opposite direction, another trolley barreled full speed toward the Niva. I heard a loud sigh from the woman behind me. "Oh, that's just great." She dropped her books on my feet. "We're all going to die now." Behind us more sparks at the wire. And then a shout from the cab in front and a terrible screeching of metal scraping against metal.

THIS WAS THE MESSAGE playing on my older brother Robert's tape recorder when my father, my wife, Maret, and I unlocked the back door of our kitchen one evening. The short, square tape recorder was held together with masking tape. It was a garage-sale reject Robert had found, and I hadn't seen the thing in several months, not since I packed it up for our move to this house. But there it was on the table, plugged in, the small spindles within the transparent viewing box turning slowly. A man's voice cracked and hissed, cut in and out,

whether because of years of smoking or because of the quality
of the tape recorder I couldn't tell.

I used to think that I would remember everything, that my
mind was the perfect tarpaper. Now I know it's not true.
Memory is a gaping yawn into which things fall, never to
return. This is how I explain it to myself, how one minute
I could be in the secret city of Gorky, the white lab coats
flapping around like angels, and then the next minute wake
up in a military hospital outside Norilsk, dust from nickel in
my lungs. And then it was as cold as the New Siberian Is-
lands, but I saw poppies everywhere, and the sea salt was so
thick in the air it crusted my eyes and nose.

"I'm dead," I said aloud, "dead or dreaming," and I
pricked my thigh with a needle a nurse had left at my bed-
side. Nothing—not a single drop of blood appeared on my
leg. I pricked myself again, harder this time. Still nothing. I
sighed, a little disappointed, but also relieved.

The winding of the spools changed in speed and we could
hear the tape laboring to its end. Then there was a sad sound
like a chainsaw's whine, and I didn't know whether it was the
man crying or the strangled noise of the tape. The recorder fell
silent. We stood there, the three of us staring at the battered
machine. Finally Dad popped open the lid and removed the
tape to read the label: "Niels, 1945."

"Who's Niels?" Maret asked.

"Who knows?" Dad slipped the tape back into the recorder. We listened to it again to see if we could hear any clues
about who this guy was or why he had left us, of all people, this
tape. Though I knew what words were coming, the hair bristled on the back of my neck when I heard them. Maret pulled
a rusted coffee can down from the cupboard and fished for her
cigarettes. After the third go-round with the tape, I shut off the
recorder.

Maret blew a jet of smoke through her nose, lifting a stray tendril of hair out of her face. "So this is supposed to be a dead guy talking to us?"

"This is somebody's sick idea of a joke," Dad said, pushing the tape recorder to the edge of the table.

"Maybe." I scratched my head, considering.

"It's this house." Dad lifted himself from his chair. But the way he spoke, it sounded like "It's his house," and that's when I decided that maybe it was. Maybe we were living in Niels's house, and Niels was who he said he was and was dead, with nothing better to do than tell us about the last moments of his life, which he himself seemed to have trouble believing.

Dad sighed. The subject of houses weighed on him. He hadn't wanted to leave our old one, the house of his children's youth, the house of his marriage. But with Robert missing for decades now and my mother dead for over a year, moving had seemed the right thing to do, at least what most people did when they sustained repeated loss. I recalled the cheer with which Mrs. Dahlstrom, our real estate agent, a tiny woman with a voice that seemed too big for her small chest, had attributed the draftiness in the hallway and kitchen to ghosts.

"Really?" Maret had asked, excited by the prospect of unexplained phenomena.

"Well," Mrs. Dahlstrom had replied, looking away, suddenly embarrassed, "there are stories. All the wrecked ships and lost people, you know." She bent her hand toward the wide windows and circled it from the wrist. Beyond her we could see the mouth of the Columbia, a huge river with treacherous currents and sandbars where it dumped into the sea. Everybody here in Astoria knew somebody who had grounded a ship on a bar or drowned while navigating a fishing boat over turbulent water. There were stories of hauntings at the shut-down tuna cannery, sightings on the docks, at the timber loaders. Stories of spirits wandering over the back roads, slick with black ice that had settled on the ground like an invisible skin. Stories, too, of people stepping into the fog and never returning.

Maret smoked another cigarette, and we left my father alone in the kitchen, standing with his hands behind his back, studying the fog thickening outside the window. I followed Maret up the stairs, my thumbs pressing into the small of her back. At the top we passed the room where we stored all of Robert's stuff, most of it still in boxes, and then turned into the room where she and I slept. Though technically the room was ours, it was so crowded with all of Mom's stuff, I felt like a visitor. Polyester batting crowded the closet, and we couldn't walk past the bed without tripping over wicker baskets and creels of thimbles, thread, needles, and scraps. Then there was her dressmaker's form, a tall, adjustable plastic-and-foam torso standing in the corner.

Though it was dark, we didn't turn on the lights. I untied my shoes, tossed them at the base of the limbless woman, and lay on the bed. Maret crawled in next to me. I ran my hands along her back, over the knobs of her spine, then around her neck and through her hair. She had thick brown hair, not especially dark or especially light, and I loved the clean soapy smell of it and the feel of it against my face. I leaned over and buried my face in it, inhaling the scent of her scalp, and wondered again how I got so lucky with her and to whom I owed this cosmic debt. For Maret had saved me, no doubt about that.

We met after Mom died. I was coasting downhill on my bike, watching a rare Swedish freighter nosing into the docks below, when I collided with the back end of her car, a red Yugo. When I came to, I was flat on my back, the exhaust pipe pumping out fumes that made me so dizzy I thought the horizon had unzipped from the hills. Above me the sandpipers and sea gulls flew belly side up, casting shadows that sailed in the opposite direction. And then I saw a woman on her hands and knees, bending over me, her eyes blue with gold spokes radiating from their dark centers. I lay there staring into those eyes.

"Say, that's a nice bike." She yanked on the hopelessly bent frame, trying to free it from the undercarriage of the Yugo.

"It's an old Mongoose—no big deal," I said, pulling myself to my feet and brushing the dirt from my pants. We took turns pulling and wrenching the frame, trying to work it free. We ended up driving over the hills and back roads, looking for potholes and rocks, anything to dislodge the bike. At last it came free on a small hill of scotch broom. But then the Yugo, possibly feeling compassion for a fellow doomed specimen, sputtered and coughed its last breath, and we ended up abandoning the car too.

"That tape," Maret whispered now in the dark, "it's weird. Who talks like that, anyway?"

"Yup," I mumbled. It was as if the man had been reading a scripted memoir about faraway places we'd never heard of and things we could hardly imagine.

"What do you think it means?" Maret asked.

"Probably nothing," I said. From a few houses up the hill a dog barked. Outside, the moon scraped a small arc in the night sky. Moonlight filtered through the gauzy curtains, turning the air in the room to the blue shades of liquid. As I listened to Maret's breathing, I reminded myself that though I could barely remember what Robert's voice sounded like, Niels was obviously an old man, and there was no way the voice I'd heard on the tape could belong to my brother. Robert would never have used a phrase like "gaping yawn," and with his nose buried in a comic book, he wasn't the type to notice electricity sparking along wires or poppies blooming out of season.

It was that time of the year when the nights were so short that a man standing in Saturday could shake hands with a man in Sunday. I checked my pockets for my passport, my papers. But they were gone. All I had left was my military card. I kept my hand in my pocket, my palm pressed against the card. As the train chuffed from Riga to Vilnius, from Vilnius to Minsk and Minsk to Smolensk, I watched the ash and paper birch give way to larch. In Nizhny Novgorod, a woman with a carp in a box boarded the train. The box had a hole cut in each end so that the head and tail stuck out, and from time to time she poured oil into the mouth of the fish. A dripping brown mess followed her as she moved from compartment to compartment. Then there was the stink.

It was Niels's habit to visit unannounced and leave us these strange accounts. Perhaps because the house had once belonged to him, he felt it necessary to lead us on these guided tours. For the next two months the tape recorder appeared once or twice a week, plugged in, a message unspooling for us as we came through the back door. The thrill of finding something, of the unexpected, incited my father to go bowling in the evening on the off-chance that Niels might visit while he was out. My father encouraged us to leave too, and so Maret and I began taking long walks to the pier, holding hands. Sometimes we made love there, and one night, walking back home, Maret even talked of having a baby, if I could quit the green chain at the mill and get a counter job at Copeland's lumberyard in Seaside while she earned her cosmetician's certificate. Those evenings, the sky didn't hang quite as low, something I had not thought possible since my brother disappeared and my mother passed away. I felt I had Niels, a complete and unexpected stranger, to thank for this renewal.

He would evidently come through the back door and smoke Maret's cigarettes. He'd leave before we returned, the nub of a cigarette dying down to ash at the bottom of the coffee can. When he smoked an entire pack during one visit, Maret wanted to file a trespassing complaint with the police, but eventually she admitted that the idea that a dead man was handling her cigarettes appealed to her sense of adventure. And then there were Niels's incredible accounts. During the war he'd fled to Romania and hidden in the *lavras,* the holy monastic caves. But he had left the caves to attend a mass in town, where he gave himself away by singing in Latin something called an Ektenia. He was discovered by soldiers attending the service and was taken to Zagreb on an open cattle car packed with other captured soldiers, many of them dying of their wounds. With them their captors had stowed a pig and an ox that had had its knees broken. What tormented him most was the dust swirling up from the ground, which stung the eyes, and his unending thirst.

In Brazil he'd seen children riding crocodiles with bridles fitted over their long snouts. The crocodiles had had their teeth pulled and had lost the will to snap, though the instinct to roll was still strong enough for the adults to stand by with stout sticks.

In Archangel he'd gotten into a face-slapping contest with a priest. When a clear victor could not be decided, the priest had stabbed Niels in the hand with a holy bird feather carved out of ice.

In Latvia he was taken for a spy and was exiled to Siberia via a barge on the wide and cold River Yenisey.

I could hear the interest rate accruing on atrocity. I noted how the frozen ground of Norilsk remained regardless of how many buildings had been built on it, and how many bones stowed beneath.

I listened, imagining steep riverbank cliffs and skeletons emerging from the earth. I tried to think what these things Niels claimed to have seen or done could possibly mean. And this was when his accounts would hit a raw nerve: I had wanted to travel, to be able to tell such stories, stories that might make other people think my life had been worth living. I turned off the recorder and carefully titled the cassette *Atrocity*. I rolled Maret's last cigarette between my thumb and forefinger and lit it with Robert's metal Zippo lighter. Then I stepped out to our back yard, determined not to let bitterness take root.

Down the sweep of the grass and jammed against the neighbors' fence was a beehive burner, a holdover from the days when Astoria had had a booming lumber business. The burner was a dome of chicken wire stretched over a frame of metal hoops. On the neighbors' roof was the most exotic landscape Astoria had to offer: two pairs of tennis shoes, a Frisbee, and what looked like the handlebar of a lawnmower. Looking at that discarded clutter, I envied Niels a little for all that he had seen—Niels, who broke the bones of this life wide open. Niels, who refused to disappear quietly.

I'd grown up in a smaller house perched dangerously on a hill. We took comfort in the fact that on either side of ours were several other houses placed just as precariously. But at night, when the wind howled through the pines and the floorboards creaked, I'd lie awake listening to Robert's flutelike snores and the unsteady sounds of the house settling on its foundation. It seemed to be always raining, and I think Mom expected the row of houses to slide down the hill at any moment. She was in the habit of measuring the distance from the back steps to the fence with the clothesline she could never use on account of the weather.

We'd lived in Astoria for as long as I could remember. When Robert was drafted in early 1970 and sent to Vietnam, I was only eight, maybe nine, still just a kid with a paper route. Robert was anxious to go; not much ever seemed to happen in Astoria except businesses relocating or shutting down for good

—the tuna and salmon canneries, the dockside granaries. Even the barges from far-off places like Finland and Japan began to sail into port less often. When Robert didn't return at the end of his tour, my parents made phone calls, wrote letters. After five years, they began slowly to resign themselves to the probability that he was dead.

Those were the long years. The sky dumped water for months on end. On the other side of the Columbia, a house actually slid down into the river. The line of dew rose steadily and clouds brewed in the tops of the spruces and pines. Those were the years in which Dad bought graphite pencils in all shades of slate and in his off-hours became a self-taught expert on the nuances of gray. We had a water pump running twenty-four seven in the basement. And every day for five years at least, as I rode my bike and delivered papers, I told myself that over the next hill, at the end of the stretch of tracks or down by the docks, if I was faithful and kept looking, Robert would step out of the fog.

Eventually the water wore Mom down—at least, that's how I explained it to myself. She stopped climbing the stairs to her sewing room and could often be found on her hands and knees, crying, in the bathroom. She stopped going to church. Then she stopped talking. Finally I came home one day from school to find her sitting in a kitchen chair, her chin touching her chest. Her heart had stopped beating.

We stayed in that house for another year, irremediably alone, my father and I like people belonging to sad and separate families. I enrolled in community college, then dropped out, reenrolled and dropped out again every term for a year before I finally wised up to myself. Dad kept on at the cannery and spent the rest of his time arranging his bowling-ball garden along the steep incline of the back yard or sitting in his recliner, his feet up and his eyes half closed. At night I could hear him talking to my mother, asking her impossible questions like how could she leave him like that and who the hell did she think she was and when was she coming back?

I'd pull on my jeans, creep down the stairs, and let myself out into the wind and rain. I'd walk up and down the narrow roads that connected these dark hills, walking my old paper route. I'd note the fuzzy yellow halos of light in certain kitchens, the pale squares illuminating the front walks of houses. I'd watch people moving from one square of light to another, and I'd imagine the happy and full lives of those people I wanted to be.

It was after a Friday bowling tournament that we had a stroke of incredible luck. While we were away, Niels had visited. When we climbed the back steps, I saw the curtains at the kitchen window move suspiciously. I pulled the door open, and at the kitchen table was a small film projector. The cord was plugged in and the light bulb switched on. On the projector's flat top sat a silver canister, the kind used for old films. I loaded the film and aimed the projector's lens at the blank patch of wall next to the back door.

Whatever lingering, irrational hope I might have had that somehow, by some incredible fortune, Niels was in actuality Robert dissolved immediately. Niels did not in the slightest resemble my brother. He was weathered and cracked, like an old wallet, his long nose dividing his face into two equal halves.

> I collect clocks—the older, the better. Some of my clocks still keep time, some don't. The ones that measure too slowly have always been my favorites, because I can imagine I am living at different speeds at the same time.

He spoke as if he'd recently lost some teeth, his mouth barely moving. When he excused himself to get a glass of water, we could see that he had been sitting on the steps of a staircase. The railing was all too familiar.

When Neils returned, a glass in hand, Maret cocked her head and studied his face. "God, he's ugly. And not in a usual way, either." Then she grunted. "Well"—she pushed back from her chair—"you can listen to only so much of that." She turned for the stairs. I watched her walk slowly up the steps, watched her head disappear, then her shoulders, her back, her legs and feet. I knew she would soon fall into a thick and dreamless sleep. Suddenly I found myself amazed at Maret's capacity to become bored by Niels. I puzzled over her indifference, and I wondered how much longer she'd find me interesting.

"He's sure in no hurry to get to the end," Dad grumbled. He stood, rubbed the palms of his hands in slow circles over his face, then went into the living room and switched on the TV. I stayed and listened to Niels and to the ratchety noise of the celluloid catching on the spindles and the calming hum of the reels turning. This film had come from a valise, which Niels referred to as his Jutland suitcase. In it he had stashed many more tapes and films, and he promised to bring us the valise whenever we liked. At this point his voice turned thick and heavy and his gaze slid to a point behind the camera. I took it that he fostered a long-held fantasy of Jutland, the Danish mainland, a place he mentioned often, though he was careful to point out that he'd never actually been there.

I sat back in the chair and watched his image flickering against the kitchen wall. I admired his uneconomical telling of his adventures. That's the problem, I thought—most people try to tell the many stories of their lives but are interrupted, time and again, until they begin to forget them. I thought about this man in front of me, who'd worked so hard with all his stories—recording his tapes and now these films. I decided then that I could never hear too much or listen too hard.

Though it was clear Niels shared himself with all of us equally, I liked to think he had a special affection for me, that he wished me alone to understand his secrets, to know him like no one else. Soon clue retrieval occupied my every waking moment. I stacked all of Niels's packages (for he soon was leaving bundles of letters and photos as well) next to Mom's wicker creels and behind the cardboard boxes of Robert's comics and baseball cards in the other room. I called in sick at the mill so many days in a row that the foreman suggested I find work I could really believe in, and if not that, then pull my head out of my ass. These were fine pieces of advice, but I resolved to redouble my efforts to understand and communicate with Niels. I slept on the downstairs couch so I wouldn't miss Niels coming through the kitchen door, and during the day I kept a telescope trained on the docks. Though I hardly moved from the couch, I had never felt so invigorated, so alive, I told myself each morning in the mirror.

"What are we if not alive?" I thumped my chest with my fist one morning.

"Dead?" Dad called up from the living room.

"Since you're in the bathroom, shave, why don't you? It's been three weeks," Maret said as she walked past the open door, her voice as tight as a fist. She had a series of beautician tests scheduled over the next several weeks, and I attributed her surliness to pre-exam jitters.

That evening during dinner, Maret picked at her food while Dad watched professional bowling on TV in the other room. I sat at the table wondering about Niels's life. Had he married or ever been in love? Did he in fact live in this house with his family? Did he have a brother who'd gone missing —was this the reason behind his wanderings and his visiting us? I knew I wasn't alone in my curiosity—Maret was peeling an orange and arranging the rinds into the shape of a man.

"If he wants us to leave this house, he should just say so." She placed a bow-shaped peel where an arm would go.

"He's getting to be a pain in the ass," Dad called from the other room.

I shrugged and watched the dark shapes of the neighbors across the street move past their living room window.

The next morning I went to the cemetery. The grass was spongy, and with every step I sank into the ground a bit. A small miracle: the sun burned through the fog. Taking it as a sign, I stayed for several hours, leaving deep footprints that immediately filled with water as I ran my hands over the wet stones. After it seemed I'd touched every stone, Mom's included, I'd found a Niels Lindstrom, a Niels Magnusson, and a Niels Becker.

That night, around one in the morning, I thought I heard Niels enter through the kitchen door, whistling.

"Robert!" Dad shouted, knocking over his nightstand.

I jumped from the couch, but by the time I got to the kitchen, all I heard was the screen door slamming and more whistling, a tune I'd never heard before. When I looked outside, no one was there. On the kitchen table I saw a package addressed to all of us by name. I opened it to find a handkerchief, red-and-white-striped rubber swimming trunks, and another packet of letters. I held the handkerchief to my nose and inhaled the sour smell of sweat, acrid like wet leather. I slipped it into my back pocket.

A few nights later, as I lay on the couch, I thought I saw the red circle of a glowing cigarette butt. But when I looked more closely, I saw it was only the taillight of a truck receding into the fog outside. After that I became restless at night, drifting from one room to another, unmoored, awash in wakeful dreaming.

An old story tells of a ship captain who saw a mermaid. No one believed him, of course. To prove he wasn't lying, each evening at sunset he rowed past the sandbar in search of her. He grew so fond of rowing over the water, feeling the buck and pitch of the waves, that he tethered himself to his seat. And though he was bound, he felt that he was soaring, his soul lighter, freed of the life that held him back. Soon he forgot why he was rowing, and one night he rowed a little farther beyond the spit, then beyond the lighthouse, and finally to the open sea, where the current took him away. The old captain didn't fight it.

Thinking about Niels was like this story, I decided one night. Why did I persist in paddling over these murky and unplumbable depths? Was there some inexplicable need for the living to know the dead and the dead to be remembered by the living? After all, Niels insisted that his stories be heard and had chosen me as his audience. At every turn he seemed to be saying to us, "Look! I am still here."

I climbed the stairs to our bedroom, where Maret lay sleeping, and kicked a clear path through the clutter so that I could stand and look out the window. The sky hung like dark bolts of cloth. The sound of the wind howling through the trees made me glad for the four walls of this room, though the windows rattled and there was a strange scraping in the flue. Perhaps it was simpler. Perhaps Niels, afraid that these hills he loved had emptied of him, had come back merely to hear the familiar sounds of his house.

I slid open the window. From higher up in the wet forests, a dog barked. I leaned my elbows on the open sill, the aluminum tracks pushing into my forearms, and I listened to that dog yodel. I pulled back from the window and fingered Niels's thin metal tags, which I now wore around my neck. My own life seemed so bare next to his, and I felt that his visits had become about more than maintaining his memory through time. Maybe he had come on a last mission to teach me how to live better.

"Will you please shut up?" Maret glared at me from the bed. I started and tripped over the dressmaker's form, unaware that I had been talking to myself.

He was writing, the king of Sweden was. But at the critical moment, I sneezed. It was a colossal sneeze and it lifted the wet letters off the page, blowing them like dandelion fluff all about the room. The king looked at his blank pages. He looked at his security officers guarding the door. Then he looked at me. In his eyes a threatening anger flared. The queen buried her face in her handkerchief and her shoulders shook, from laughter or tears—I couldn't quite tell.

This was the tape Niels had left for us to find when we came back from coffee at Pig in a Pancake. Maret hadn't been sleeping well. She had dark circles under her eyes, and when she saw the tape recorder propped up on the kitchen table, she grabbed her binder full of color wheels of dyed hair swatches, backed out the door, and pulled it closed with a loud bang.

There was a long pause on the tape. Dad walked through the kitchen and to his chair in front of the TV.

"Where do our words go once they've been spoken?" Niels asked.

The tiny reels spun, the tape creaking as it wound around the spindles. I felt a chill start at the base of my neck and travel to my tailbone. It was the first time I heard Niels's voice falter, and I detected a threadbare desperation, bewilderment too, as if death had clearly disappointed him. I rubbed my palms together and blew on my hands.

Niels sighed loudly.

"The habit of living is the hardest to break," he said at last. "Now each evening I watch the sun sink into the horizon until all that is left is carmine and cobalt hovering over the rise, taking the last flash of day. I walk toward the sun, but a man from the power and water authority always stops me. 'It's God's,' he says. 'Don't try to steal his light.' "

Here a coughing fit seized Niels, and I imagined him extinguishing the last of Maret's cigarettes in the coffee can. "We are nothing without a mystery!" Niels shouted, and the tape whined to a halt.

Maret threw up around the clock for twenty-four hours. "Morning sickness?" I asked hopefully as I held her hair back when she kneeled in front of the toilet. "Just nerves," she said with a withering glance. She'd passed the N-series of hair-dye mixing, but she still had to pass the last exam: a cut, streak, and perm on a live subject. "I can't afford to screw this up," she moaned as I carried six-packs of soda water up to our bedroom and let Niels's bundles of shoes, letters, and trinkets pile up on the kitchen table.

After a few days she seemed to recover. She sat up in bed one morning, her back straight and her eyes clear. I sat next to her. "You can't keep on like this," she said, pressing a finely honed red fingernail into my chest. With a flick of her finger and thumb, she set Niels's dog tags jangling. "He's like unclaimed baggage revolving endlessly around a conveyor."

I looked at the closet stuffed with batting and yarn and tried to think of something to say.

"In your heart you aren't here with me. And I need you, Jerry." Maret's voice was as small as it could get.

I looked into her eyes, and by the curve of her eyebrows, the shape of her lips, the feel of her thin white hands in mine I was reminded of how beautiful she was. I could see also how easily I could lose her if I wasn't careful.

That night I packed up the tape recorder, the projector. There was nothing I could do if Niels continued to leave letters or photos. We locked the back door and Maret moved the coffee can to the upstairs bathroom.

For two weeks Niels did not visit, and I began to believe we had shaken him off for good. Maret brightened visibly with every night that passed without another tape or reel appearing on the kitchen table. She was happier these days: she'd aced her exam, and out of a pool of more than fifty applicants for an opening in Seaside, she'd been called back for an interview.

I, however, was miserable. Each morning I awoke, read the classifieds, and made phone calls. I drifted aimlessly from room to room, looking at Niels's tapes, photos, and letters. I worried that we had hurt him.

One night in early spring when the weather lifted, Niels returned. We came back from bowling and on the table was Robert's tape recorder, plugged in and turned on. We sat, our bowling bags at our feet, our chalked fingers laced in our laps, and listened.

The sea turned hard into buckles of ice. The salt crystallized into diamonds on the uneven surface of the water. I walked for hours, the sun overhead beating down, my eyes blinded by the glare.

"Water, water everywhere, and not a drop to drink," I muttered, tripping over the deep furrows of ice. I would walk until I reached the end of the world, the line where sea and sky are said to meet. But as I walked I saw that such a line did not exist. In the distance a woman lay on her side, encrusted in the ice. She was propped up on an elbow and smiling brilliantly, as if she were not feeling an ounce of pain. She waved me forward, calling me by name.

"I'm dead," I whispered into her hair.

"Yes," she said, still smiling.

I thought of tweezers, of splinters. Every inch of my skin itched. Is this how it ends, I wondered, feeling your own diminishment as itch gains upon itch? I imagined hundreds of tiny and quiet deaths gathering in my joints, knuckling down my back to my heels.

"Turn it off, Jerry!" Dad's face had turned crimson, and he slapped his palm against the table. "Turn it off, I said!" He rose so suddenly that his chair tipped over onto its back.

The next day Maret woke early and left for school without a word. Dad and I avoided each other most of the day. At twilight I heard his heavy footfalls on the staircase.

He stood for a moment outside our bedroom, his arms folded across his chest. "We gotta move this junk out of here," he said, motioning his head toward the sloping stacks of letters and photos and the boxes of trinkets. "Comes a spark, a short circuit, and the whole house'll burn to the ground."

He was right. The room was beginning to look like an antique shop, a tired landscape of neglected things: buttons, an old bike, a bowler hat, photos, the rubber swimming trunks, one of those heavy iron curling balls Dad used to push around on the ice when he was a kid. Shed skins, casings, and trappings.

I shoved a box sideways with my foot. Then I went to the room where Robert's things were stored. I carried shoeboxes of letters down the stairs and through the kitchen and down the back steps and stacked them in the open bed of Dad's truck. Then I went back for Robert's tape recorder, the film projector, the tapes, the many reels of drooping film.

Back into the house I went, returning a minute later with the gramophone, then the curling ball, the swimming trunks, the old bike, and, though I hated to do it, the endless stacks of faded photographs, every person bleached to a ghost. Finally I unfolded the handkerchief from my back pocket, removed the tags from around my neck, and tossed them onto the mound. *A clean sendoff,* I said to myself, and after I lit a cigarette with Robert's Zippo lighter, I tossed the lighter in too.

I heard Dad laboring down the back steps, his heavy tread on the grass. He had a pair of thick work gloves on, and under one arm he carried the plastic torso of Mom's dressmaker's form. Around the waist he'd tied some of Mom's scarves, and in his other hand he carried the wicker creels of buttons and zippers. He eased the dressmaker's form over the wheel well, then let it drop with a loud *thunk* onto the bed. Overhead the moon cast a damp light that transformed the bowling pins in the yard into stately markers, the wooden shapes of women. Dad followed my gaze. Then he upended the pins, one by one. He cradled them in his arms and carried them to the truck, where he pitched them in.

We trudged upstairs. It took only a few minutes to empty our room of everything except the bed and Maret's and my things. Then, by unspoken agreement, we began emptying the other room: Robert's suitcases of clothes, his comic-book collection, his baseball trading cards, all his drafting pencils and paper. By the time Maret came home, we'd completely filled the truck bed. We climbed into the front, with Maret squeezed between us, and drove slowly, the truck heavy with the weight. As we drove down the empty roads, past the museum of an old ship captain, past the old jail, we dropped into a thick bank of fog. We were headed to the docks, the place people went to get rid of things.

We idled past the loader and the boom crane, making sure no one was there to see us. We looked long and hard, as the fog had a way of fooling people and we all knew of joyriders who had mistaken water for solid ground. Dad stopped the truck, and I hopped out of the cab, lowered the tailgate, then climbed back in. "Ready?" Dad looked at us. With a whoop, Maret braced her feet on the dash. Then Dad ground on the shifter and the truck lurched into reverse. Cold air rushed through the cab, and I gritted my teeth, gripping the granny handle for all I was worth. As we flew past the loader, Dad slammed on the brakes. I whipped my head around just fast enough to watch momentum clean out the truck bed in one smooth haul. Over the edge of the dock all the stuff went flying, landing with a loud splash in the water below.

Dad and I got out of the cab and stood shoulder to shoulder, studying the water without speaking. I folded my arms across my chest. I realized that not since Mom's funeral had I stood this close to my father.

Behind me I heard Maret roll down the window. I stepped closer to the edge of the dock. I watched the more buoyant items, like Mom's wicker baskets and her dressmaker's form, bob for a moment before disappearing beneath the cover of water.

"It's beautiful," Dad said. "A goddamn beautiful sight."

"Yes," I agreed, growing sick of all the fog and the darkness. I looked at Dad, then at Maret leaning out of the cab. I suddenly wanted to live until I used life up, ran it dry and left it with a shudder or a shout.

Halves of a Whole

ALL HER LIFE Lucy thought in halves. Upstairs, where Lucy and her family lived in tiny rooms, the Ivanyks could have been like any other family who immigrated from Hungary to the U.S. Her father oiled the Christmas carp in the bathtub until it wouldn't drink anymore, while her mother dreamed of growing a real garden, if only their back yard weren't a swatch of asphalt with just enough space for their stretch hearse. Downstairs, where her parents ran their business, the dead lay in wait. The living and the dead. A neat and certain division, as clear as the differences between herself and her twin sister, Estera. Everyone knew from the moment they were born—when Estera broke her mother's water and rushed headlong into this world, while Lucy followed slowly, cautiously, with her feet first, as if testing the air—that as identical twins they couldn't be less alike. With eyes wide open, Estera swallowed all the noise of that overly bright hospital room and gave it back in wails and energetic screams that turned her tiny face violet. But Lucy, her body pale blue, held her breath and for two days refused to open her eyes. Over the course of the next year they both acquired their mother's dark hair, and their gray eyes deepened to a brown so dark and luminous it suggested some

sort of interior vision. But once they started walking, everyone—the aunts and uncles, even Cousin Rudy, who was le-
gally blind—could tell them apart. In all the girls did and everywhere they went, Lucy lagged behind Estera and walked
with the slightest of limps. It was to be expected, a natural
extension of lingering too long inside her mother's body,
Grandmother Yeta explained, with a touch to Lucy's brow.
These words told Lucy she was marked in a way that Estera
wasn't—Estera, who was, in her father's words, high-strung;
Estera, who, according to her mother, had almost too much life
for one body, a quality that Lucy in time credited to the extra
oxygen her sister received as she tumbled too quickly into this
world.

By the time they started elementary school, their mother
had already taught them to read, using brochures and magazines sent by the American Undertakers' Association, and their
father had shown them how to use a calculator and how to
transfer calls from the upstairs to the downstairs. The chores
were part of a larger lesson they were learning: eventually
they'd take their place alongside their parents and work in service of the dead. That was their parents' Plan. After high school
the girls would go to embalming school and meet nice boys,
possibly brothers—maybe even twins. Well schooled in grief
management, end-of-life financial planning, the psychology of
casket salesmanship, their husbands would have winsome
smiles—sincere, but not overly earnest. They'd have children
who would inherit the mysterious gift of knowing when to
nudge a box of tissues closer to an elbow, when to crack a window, offer iced tea, or leave the room quietly. They would
know what people expected or needed before they knew it
themselves.

And this was the most important lesson their parents were
teaching Lucy and Estera: the gift of anticipation. So many of

life's surprising and startling pains could be dampened if only one learned to anticipate, their parents thought. But it was a dark gift, requiring a steady cultivation of fear, an ability to imagine the worst and plan to accommodate it. It was why the inscription on the back of the crucifixes the girls always wore read, *I am a Catholic, please call a priest.* Why long ago their father had purchased a family plot at Hillside, where their feet would point east so that when they were resurrected, they'd jump to their final glory and greet God face to face. It was also why at night, as they climbed into their matching beds and said prayers for the bodies waiting down below, their mother in turn prayed for them, so that they might avoid the jiltings and snubbings childhood held for girls as special as they were. "Special, meaning strange?" Estera sometimes asked. "Special, meaning called," their mother always answered, bending close to kiss them each on the forehead. When she did, a thick smell settled over them and made their eyes water.

"She wears too much perfume," Lucy said once.

"That's not perfume. That's formaldehyde," Estera corrected her.

Listening to the top twenty on her little yellow earphones was Estera's way of putting herself to sleep. It was Lucy's habit, however, to lie as motionless as possible and listen to the wind move the leaves of the plum trees outside their window. When Estera's breathing from the next bed deepened to an even tempo, Lucy would sometimes close her eyes and think about the dead, lying still and alone in the dark. These were the nights when Lucy might slip out of bed with a terrible sense that something had been overlooked. Down to the basement she'd go, grabbing a fistful of salt on the way. Though she'd been taught to tent sheets over the faces of the dead so the weight of the cloth would not crush their noses, she would turn the sheets down to their shoulders and rub salt behind their ears. Sometimes she'd pry open fingers clutched at the breast in prayer, deposit a little mound of salt in the palm for luck, and press the fingers closed again.

She'd sit through entire nights like that, waiting with the dead. Sitting there in the quiet, controlled chill of the basement, touching their hands with hers, she cared for them in ways she worried no one had for years. She found and fixed the little details her mother or father might have missed: a strand of hair out of place, a bit of fingernail polish lapped over a cuticle. These were small things she could give to these people, loving gestures they would not know or miss but, in Lucy's mind, necessary all the same.

What could it hurt, she asked herself, if she played them the top twenty or told them stories of the mischief she and Estera got into at the Jesuit high school: changing seats in English class, swapping instruments in band class? Why shouldn't these people hear about the times when Estera, trapped into dates with boys she didn't like, convinced Lucy to switch places with her, toss her hair and laugh in the throaty way Estera normally did? It was easy enough to fool the teachers, the elderly nuns, who rarely noticed students if they weren't getting into trouble. But somehow those boys that Estera didn't want and Lucy sometimes did always caught on. It was her slight limp, she figured, that hesitation in her left foot as it lifted from the ground. She wished in her heart she were really identical to her sister, could shake off that limp and laugh with ease. A crazy wish, she knew, bending to the bodies and whispering, for how much more identical could they possibly get?

After these long nights in the basement, Lucy, tired and cramped, would walk slowly in the mornings, her legs stiff and her limp more pronounced. Always, it seemed, these were the days that the kids at school made fun of her. The boys teased her, mimicking the dead with their tongues hanging out the sides of their mouths, arms held at stiff right angles to their torsos. Lucy knew they'd never seen real rigor mortis as she had. They couldn't know how it seized the body, starting in the face, around the mouth, and spread downward. They couldn't know that a body went completely limp three or four hours later, or the importance of working quickly to remove any pooled blood before it settled as long bruises in the lower limbs. Knowing these things made it easy for Lucy to dismiss the boys. But the girls were harder to ignore. While changing for PE, some would imitate her walk while others would offer to set her up with their homely younger brothers. Lucy always ended up hiding in a stall in the girls' locker room. Magically, mercifully, the door of the stall next to hers would whine on its hinges and the lock would slide. Then she'd hear Estera's voice: *Don't cry, they'll hear you.*

"Presentation is everything" was the Ivanyk family motto. You could be dying—dead—they'd joke privately, as long as you looked good. That's what people cared about the most. The toughest preparations were victims of accidents involving the loss of limbs, fires, or drowning. Trauma deaths spelled a lot of head, face, and neck work with paraffin and makeup. In the event of strangulation or decapitation, the Ivanyks placed a red filter over the track lights in the chapel to cast a rosy glow over the casket. Usually Mrs. Ivanyk would dress the deceased with a scarf or high collar, for in such deaths it seemed the neck was the first place everyone looked.

Equally tricky were jaws and mouths, the places where people carried their stress.

"Look to the lips," Mrs. Ivanyk told them the day they finished their third-year final exams at high school. She peeled back the lower lip of Mrs. Rand, a serious woman who had lived down the street and distributed religious literature instead of candy at Halloween. They hadn't yet inserted the plastic eye caps, and with Mrs. Rand's shrunken eyes still open and her gaze trained on the ceiling, Lucy wondered if she was even now glimpsing the beyond described in her four-step salvation tracts.

"See"—her mother pointed with a needle at the woman's lip—"that's the weather line." There were two halves to the lip, one side rough, still colored with lipstick, the other side smooth, filmed with mucus. Her mother nodded at the head shot tacked to the wall, which Mrs. Rand's family had provided for reference. "Sometimes those photos aren't detailed enough, so you have to look carefully at the face for the clues. This weather line tells how she held her mouth and how to glue it closed and where to apply lipstick." Mrs. Ivanyk grimaced and massaged the tight jaw muscles. "She should have smiled more," she said, threading the needle with horsehair. With a few quick bobs through a nostril, her mother pulled the corners of the mouth. "There," she said, and now Mrs. Rand, her hands folded on her chest, looked as if she'd stumbled onto their worktable and into a deep sleep and might at any moment awake, bewildered but well rested.

Estera dabbed a thin blue mustache of VapoRub above her own upper lip to combat the powerful smell of the embalming agent. "That's good, but we could make her look better," she said. She picked a different shade of lip liner and drew a careful outline. Then she feathered a lighter shade of lipstick over Mrs. Rand's chapped lips. When she was done, Lucy had to admit that Mrs. Rand did look better.

Their mother took the tacks from the photo and held it to Mrs. Rand's face, comparing the two faces. "No," she pronounced at last. "We go by the photo." Estera turned without a word and went upstairs to the office, where Lucy knew she'd answer phones too abruptly and file away at her fingernails until they were nothing but blunted nubs.

· · ·

That night, while Lucy combed out her hair, she stood behind her sister at the vanity. It was their nightly ritual, and the time they said the things they'd been saving up for each other during the day. Tonight Lucy thought that with the movements of their brushes and combs so even and smooth, so synchronized, they didn't even need words to understand each other.

Estera, finished with her brush, picked up a tube of apricot lipstick. She colored her lips, then blew an imaginary kiss at Lucy's reflection in the mirror.

"What was that for?" Lucy asked.

"For luck. Or maybe for nothing. Or maybe I was just practicing."

Lucy felt her brows meeting in the middle of her forehead; she simply did not know what to think.

Estera laughed. "Oh, I forgot. You've never been kissed." She turned and clasped Lucy's hands in hers. Then she pulled Lucy close and kissed her hard on the mouth. Confused, Lucy struggled, but Estera held her tight. Just when Lucy thought she could no longer breathe, Estera moved her mouth to Lucy's ear. "That's a kiss," Estera said, releasing her. "And I can tell you right now, you could use some practice." Estera laughed again and switched off the light.

Lucy crawled into bed and lay very still, feeling small and stupid and embarrassed. She listened to the insects pinging against the wire screens. She traced the outline of her mouth with her fingers and wondered where and with whom Estera had learned to kiss like that.

They buried Mrs. Rand the next morning, and the funeral for a toddler murdered by the mother's live-in boyfriend was scheduled for that evening. Certain hurts, Lucy was beginning to see, outstripped words and by necessity afforded certain privileges. Which was why the Ivanyks had a policy not to discuss with the survivors how their loved one had died. After all, these people—that mother kneeling now in front of the quarter-sized casket, for example—were here not to dwell on the details but to create for themselves a better ending to a bad story.

That evening it was a rushed service. As the memorial for the child concluded and the family congregated in the hall-way, Lucy could hear the fax machine stuttering and humming with the coroner's death certificate. They'd been waiting for this fax, couldn't bury the baby without it, and one of Estera's jobs was to rush it out to the priest at Hillside before the family motorcade arrived. But Estera wasn't in the office.

Lucy threaded her way through the mourners and headed upstairs, where she found her sister slumped at the vanity, her face held between her fists. She was crying. Lucy supposed she was upset about the child, too young to leave this world, not even having had a chance to know it.

"Shhhh—they'll hear you!" Lucy said, handing Estera a tis-sue. With a savage swipe, Estera removed all traces of her tears and repaired her eyeliner and mascara so quickly that if Lucy had not been there, had not seen Estera crying, she'd never have believed it.

Lucy bent to the window and watched the family disband outside and the mother climb into the lead car. "It's sad, that baby."

"What baby?" Estera recapped her eyeliner.

Lucy squinted. "The one we're loading up in the hearse. The one whose death certificate you're supposed to be deliver-ing right now."

"Oh, yeah." Estera slid off the stool and steadied herself with a hand at the vanity.

"What's the matter with you?"

But Estera shook her head. "It's just nerves," she said, brush-ing past Lucy.

. . .

Mindful of the importance of props, Mrs. Ivanyk was careful to leave the women and children with their hands upturned, a chunk of ice in each palm for luck. Having learned the trade in Hungary under Grandmother Yeta's tutelage, she had a sharp understanding of the rules governing the dead and their particular needs: hyssop, geranium seeds, pickled nasturtium stems, salt—you could never give too much salt. Salt was ballast, salt the tears, the substitute for flimsy words and threadbare grieving. And if you ran out, and even sometimes if you didn't, it was important to secure the bodies with alternate cargo. On this score Lucy had seen almost everything: caskets cluttered with beer cans—some full, some not—extra pairs of shoes stowed by the feet, the collars of beloved household pets perched in the crook of an elbow.

The body itself was, of course, the most important prop, which was why at Ivanyks' they asked their clients to bring their loved ones' prosthetics, dentures, and wigs to the consultations. On this muggy August evening, Lucy's mother and father were down to the last consultation. It was a sad case: a thirty-year-old woman taken by breast cancer.

Her father shook his head slowly from side to side as Mrs. Talley, the dead woman's mother, and the woman's two grown daughters came in. "Grass is a sorry thing when it's growing from the bed of a river," her father said, his gaze trained out the window. Half a mile away was a drying-up riverbed.

"Too little rain, the story we all know," Mrs. Talley returned, matching the rhythm of Mr. Ivanyk's headshakes with her own pitch and roll. The Talleys were Lithuanians and had come from a land of cemeteries. Lucy figured they'd be veteran grievers. Which was why their sudden bickering caught her by surprise. The mother and daughters couldn't agree on whether they wanted Lucy to dress the deceased with her mastectomy bra, its padded breasts sewn into the cups.

"Barbara would have wanted to have looked normal," said the older daughter, a woman with buckteeth the color of almonds. Lucy took one look and knew her dentition would be serious work for an embalmer someday.

"How do you know what she would have wanted?" Mrs. Talley snapped the jaws of her purse closed.

"It's not like they grew back," the younger daughter said. "I think we need to be *real* about all of this." Her eyes searched the room for validation and settled on Lucy, who felt her face flush. She dropped her gaze to her shoes. Even though Barbara Talley was tucked away downstairs, Lucy was glad she had already glued the woman's eyelids closed so that she could not see her family now.

Later, after the three women argued over casket selection and left in separate cars, refusing to speak to one another, Lucy wheeled Barbara into the prep room. She placed a hand on her forehead, ran a finger along her temples, half expecting to feel the faint beat of a pulse. Barbara's head seemed too large for her shrunken body, as if she were dreaming dreams too grand, and despite the fresh bloom of purple bruising along her cheeks, she looked beautiful in a way Lucy couldn't pinpoint.

In their room that night, Lucy sank to her bed, dizzy. She didn't know if after all these years the embalming fluids had finally gotten to her, or if it was the August heat. Estera emptied the contents of the vanity drawers on the floor and tossed old eyebrow pencils and lip liners one by one into the small metal trash can. "All that over a brassiere," Estera said as a compact of blusher landed at the bottom of the can with a loud clunk. "The sad thing is that they really think it makes a difference."

"It does, though," Lucy said, opening the window and sliding back the screen. "It's the last look that everyone remembers." She leaned over the sill and smelled the river drying, a smell like rotting fish or bad weather. And she breathed in other smells: the chemicals from Chase's Beauty School at the end of the street, burned dust.

"From now on, each morning we should just flip a coin. Heads we only talk to living people that day. Tails we talk to the dead." Estera laughed. "Because, I swear, looking at those Talley women, I just wanted to fix their makeup or something. And listening to them made me want to quit entirely."

Lucy swallowed. "You can't quit."

Estera wiped her hands along her thighs, then riffled though an open magazine on her bed. "I could be a food stylist. After all, they do a lot of the same things we do." She pointed to an ad. "I bet you didn't know that this Butterball turkey isn't even cooked. A food stylist peels back a thin little piece and cooks that one slice with a hair dryer until it looks done. Then they paint the skin brown. The rest of the turkey is actually still frozen."

"Where do you hear about these things?"

"While you're setting faces, I'm in the office reading." Estera smiled and flipped to another ad.

"You can't quit," Lucy said again. Quitting was absolutely not part of their parents' Plan, which determined that nobody went anywhere but here.

A strange smile drifted over Estera's face. "Have you ever wondered what it would be like if one of us were gone?" She reached into her purse and withdrew a cigarette. Lucy had never seen Estera smoke before and watched her strike the match, the flame illuminating her face.

"You mean like if we were separated?" This was a suggestion so unthinkable that Lucy could hardly say the words.

"No. Gone. As in not alive," Estera said, the cigarette bobbing between her lips.

"It's bad luck to talk about dying," Lucy said at last, "unless it's business."

Estera shrugged and flicked the match out the window.

Lucy leaned on the sill again, her eyes following the flight of
the spent match into the tomato plants.

When Estera switched off the lights, Lucy climbed into bed
and lay flat on her back. She thought of Barbara below in the
dark of their basement and placed a palm over her left breast.
Barbara had been diagnosed too late for the doctors to be able
to do much. She'd lived for years with cancer, according to the
medical records. The possibility that a lump of flesh could betray her, that death could cocoon as a clutch of cells and wait
patiently, like a moth, for the right moment to hatch and unfurl
its wings, disturbed her. Lucy could not fall asleep for fear that
such a thing had already happened, that she or her sister already
had some hidden illness they didn't yet know about.

Over the following days and weeks, Lucy felt a terrible pre-
science, a certainty that something bad would happen. Their
cousin Rudy, a man with weak eyes but a good heart, died suddenly of a heart attack, and she was sure more bad news was on
the way. McLeod's Family Funerary Services and Silverman's
Mortuary from across town called to offer their condolences
and to offer complete embalming and facial sets, a gesture all
the Ivanyks appreciated, but the unspoken rule among family
morticians was that they prepared their own dead.

"Who will be next?" Estera wondered aloud the night after
they'd prepped the chapel for Rudy's funeral. "After all, death
travels in pairs," she said, giving Lucy a knowing look. "Everyone dies, it's just that some people work harder at it than others," Lucy wanted to say, for she had detected several perplex-
ing new habits Estera had adopted. There was the smell of
wine on Estera's breath, and her returning home later and later
in the evenings, long after her night class on grief counsel-
ing had let out. Then there was the way she sometimes pressed
her thumbs into her temples or stopped to catch her balance

against doorframes. And then there was that strange crying jag the day of the toddler's burial.

Singly each observation meant nothing, but Lucy couldn't help adding it all up. Estera was living life recklessly. Or maybe she was living life abundantly, living life the way you would when you were dying and had nothing left to lose. "Whatever it is, you can tell me," Lucy felt like saying. "It's not for nothing that we're twins." Whatever afflicted her sister, real or imagined, Lucy would gladly support her so that Estera would not have to carry it alone. But knowing that Estera would probably not tell her even if she did ask was too much to take, and Lucy began walking with her shoulders caved in, her body a question mark.

"Don't slouch," her mother warned one evening while they were taking inventory of the stockroom. It was her mother's way of reminding Lucy how difficult it was to work the brittle backs of old women, her way too of reminding Lucy that with her limp and her decidedly mousy ways, she could not afford to add bad posture to her list of flaws. Lucy trudged upstairs, her left foot slapping the steps hard. Later, from the window, she turned her eyes toward the stars and waited for her sister to come home.

Estera left the basement door ajar or unlocked almost every night now, and Lucy, not wanting her sister to get caught, left it that way. Their mother and father asked Lucy a lot of questions about Estera. Did Lucy think she was up to something? Whose cigarette butts cluttered the tomato plants? Was Estera seeing someone?

"Beats me," Lucy would say with a shrug. She was almost certain Estera had a boyfriend. Still, Lucy was bothered by the things her sister would not share with her. And then there were the dark circles under Estera's eyes, which Lucy had just noticed with surprise, for it was Estera who had shown her how to hide fatigue by fanning tiny dots of foundation along the hollow just under the lower eyelids. "The chemicals sap my color," Estera explained. And the muscle aches and cramps she complained about? "Just ordinary female trouble," Estera would say with a wave of her hand, batting away all future questions.

One night, when the moon was a sliver, Lucy sat at the end of her bed and observed Estera. "Are you OK?" Lucy finally asked. "Because you look a little different. Tired, maybe."

"I'm fine. But you," Estera said, snapping her textbook shut, "need a social life."

"I don't know," Lucy said. She was as social as she wanted to be, spending her days with dozens of Barbaras and Mrs. Rands. She was learning that the dead were less work than the living. You could screw up big and it didn't matter. The dead would forgive, waiting patiently for their repairs.

"You could be cute," Estera said. "I don't get it. You're as good with makeup as I am. Maybe better. But look at you." Lucy stood behind her sister at the vanity and squinted. Estera, with her long black hair and her strong Hungarian jaw, was beautiful, as pretty as any of the models in those magazines she was always reading. And Lucy knew it wasn't for nothing that they were twins. She could be pretty too. Maybe even go out with a good Catholic boy. But the features she shared with her sister looked handed down, as if Lucy were made up of the leftover parts. The sisters were like two halves of a whole: Estera the beginning, the source, and Lucy her belated echo. And somehow Lucy knew it would always be this way. Thinking of how she'd always struggle to catch up, she grew afraid.

"Are you going to leave me?" she asked, her eyes locked on her sister's in the mirror.

"We're tired," Estera said. "We should just go to bed."

• • •

Lucy had developed a plan in which she and Estera would out-live their husbands. They'd spend their inheritances frugally, tucking away what they could for their children, who would one day have children of their own. Lucy had always figured that she and Estera would die on the same day, only in a differ-ent order from their birth. Lucy would go first—freed from her vexing limp at last—and Estera, making as much noise as she could, would follow. This had to be what Jesus was talking about when he said the first shall go last and the last first.

So the next morning, when Estera wouldn't get out of bed, and later, when her mother went to rouse her and couldn't, Lucy thought Estera was playing a prank on them. This had to be just her sister's powers of practical joking. Even as her mother called the priest, Lucy thought that at any second Estera would leap from the bed. The horrible moment when she realized that Estera was not joking stopped her cold. Then came her mother's shrieks and her father's sobs and frayed keening. When her mother's voice gave out, she pinched a forefinger and a thumb and drew the sign of the cross over Es-tera's forehead with small strokes. Then she rubbed salt in Es-tera's ears and candle wax on her lips, asking Estera the ques-tions for which there were no available answers: "How?" and "Why?"

In a daze, Lucy listened to her parents make the hard phone calls to the family physician, the coroner's office. Soon after, the phone rang with condolences: McLeod's and Silverman's with offers to help, and then the New Jersey relatives in conference with the Galveston relatives. For five hours the phone did not stop ringing, and after the coroner examined Estera, now laid out in the basement, Lucy put extra candle wax in her sister's ears so she could sleep better through all that would happen to her next.

Lucy stood beside her sister and hoped that little thoughts might still be firing—possibly, somehow—between the neurons deep inside Estera's head. As long as Estera was laid out on the stainless steel table, Lucy could pretend she was playing one of her old pranks, reserved for the first-day interns sent over from the embalming school across town. Or she could pretend that Estera was sleeping, that she was having a bad day and was just resting. Lucy could tell herself any number of things as long as she didn't watch her father and mother, now finished with the phone and pulling on their latex gloves and work aprons. She knew she shouldn't be surprised that they wanted to work fast. After all, she had seen how heat could unbind flesh from bone, and already Estera's skin and muscles were undergoing changes. This is what she told herself as her father hooked up the aspirator and switched on the pump. As he bent his head to his shoulder, as he rested a hand on Estera's arm, and as he picked up the trocar. He was not hurting her, she reminded herself, and nothing ever would again.

Lucy turned for the stairs. Tears streamed down her face, made her vision blurry and her steps uncertain. The pump was set on auto, and with every flush Lucy couldn't help imagining her beautiful sister broken down to bits: first her liver, then her lungs, and finally the separate chambers of her heart. It seemed wrong that Estera should so quickly be carried off to the underground world of the sewers. And as Lucy climbed up and down the stairs, breathing in time to the uneven movement of her feet and the sounds of the pump, she wished a number of crazy things: That she could whirl time backward in order to prevent this thing from happening. That she could trade places so that it was she instead of her sister laid out on the worktable. And if not these things, that she could wrap each portion of her sister in packing paper and address these little bundles to each of the family saints with a note attached: *This is my sister, and this, and this. Take better care of her.*

When she knew there couldn't possibly be anything left of

Estera to remove, when she could think of no other crazy things she could or couldn't have done, Lucy stopped climbing up and down the stairs. Sitting on the bottom step, she studied the long form of her sister's body hoisted now in the harness. Her father was upstairs in the shower, pounding his fists against the walls. Her mother had taken off her gloves and was struggling to get the plaid skirt of Estera's school uniform up over her hips. "It won't fit," she said at last.

Lucy ran through a mental check of all her sister's clothes hanging in their closet and knew that none of them were the kind that gave at the waist, none would accommodate the bloating that came with embalming.

"Maybe I could let out a seam." Her mother tucked her index finger into the waistband of the skirt and felt for the darts. "After all, she was such a good student. She should be buried in her uniform."

Lucy shook her head, amazed at how much her mother had missed this last year, amazed too at the sudden fury it could ignite in her. "She wasn't that good," she said, resolving to say things she had vowed never to tell her mother. Estera had betrayed the Ivanyks' Plan so swiftly, so completely, and Lucy was left now, alone and lopsided. And angry. Well seasoned by exposure to others' losses, she hadn't thought she'd ever feel the steep and sudden anger she'd heard others describe in her father's office. And she was surprised to discover that in her anger, she could even be cruel. Something perverse in her wanted to set the record straight, to shake her mother until her tongue rattled and tell her that Estera had been a horrible student, had smoked like a chimney, and probably had had sex with some good Catholic boy, she'd bet money on it now. And then, just as quickly as her anger had flared, it vanished. Where just a few seconds before it had pulsed behind her temples, now there was nothing.

"I can't do this," her mother said. Then, more quietly, "Help me." And Lucy knew she had to. Calling McLeod's or Silverman's was out of the question. Nobody knew better than Lucy how Estera would have wanted to look.

"All right," Lucy said, stepping beside her mother, "I'll do it." While her mother went upstairs to change her clothes and prepare for the arrival of family, Lucy inched the uniform over Estera's hips. Then she lowered the hoist and set Estera's jaw and mouth. She bent over her sister and brushed on the beige Kalon foundation in even layers. Twice she had to stop and repair her work because her tears had spilled onto Estera's face. Lucy was sorry for being angry, and she wanted to tell her sister so as she dabbed at her forehead with a foam sponge. Sorry for not paying closer attention to her. "It should be me here on this table," she wanted to say. "Me with my all-too-visible frailties, me with my limping foot."

Lucy dusted blusher along Estera's cheekbones. Then she teased and sprayed her sister's hair the way she would have insisted, using half a can of hairspray to hold it in place. From her pocket she withdrew red strings in varying lengths and tied them around Estera's wrists as reminders of the messages for Grandma Yeta, Grandfather Lazlo, Cousin Rudy, the good words to put in for the family members who remained behind. When she finished, she narrowed her eyes and examined her work. It wasn't perfect, but then nothing ever was in the end: not people, not the things they said or the promises they uttered, not the plans they made.

Later, in the chapel, Lucy unfolded chairs, careful to slide a package of tissues under each one. She pulled open the curtains, let the daylight flood through the glass. Her mother and her aunt Sophia, Rudy's mother, were in the kitchen at work on the three-day feast. Aunt Sophia was cursing the overripe tomatoes with the skins stretched so tight they looked like they were about to split. Her mother berated the cabbage leaves for wilting too soon, her knife hitting hard on the cutting board. Lucy tipped her head, listening to the sounds of two sisters taking turns being angry and then sorry.

In the hallway were the sounds of her father's footsteps and the quiet glide of well-oiled wheels. Then came the casket, and her father behind it, pushing. A top-of-the-line silver casket with gold handles and a golden treadle pump, it was their very best and would probably take two years at least to pay off. The shine of the closed lid forced Lucy's eyes shut. What had made her so sure that life would be what she expected? Sure that the quiet tragedies that befell so many others wouldn't visit her family?

She opened her eyes. "I'm just going out for a minute," she called to no one in particular. Though the bulletins needed collating, the spare beds needed making, and still more chairs needed unfolding, Lucy let herself be pulled outside to the dust and the heat.

"Don't go," her mother called from the kitchen. "I need you here." But Lucy stepped onto the porch anyway, feeling a plain and simple sorrow, but relief too. How could she feel both at once? she wondered, unsure which would win out over time. She knew, having memorized the grief literature, that she would be stuck in shock and denial for at least another three days, would then be pulling out her hair in grief. She should hide this obscene feeling of relief, she thought, for nowhere in all their grief literature were there any hints at the presence of such lightness and buoyancy.

Overhead the sky was a heat-mottled blue, and the ground was gray. Behind the row of houses across the street she could see the wind lifting a spiral of dirt. She licked her palm and held it up to a current of wind. Then she gripped the thin handrail beside her, feeling the vibrations of the traffic moving along the street flowing from the metal into her fingers.

She stepped off the porch and onto the top step. She could keep walking. It would be as easy as that. She took another step. Whether she was propelled by release or sorrow didn't matter now, only that she was propelled, and she could see how the two overlapped, had almost become the same. You could easily mistake one for the other. And if she imagined she was her sister, then she would have confidence in what she was feeling, what she was doing: right foot down, left foot down —this was what Estera would have wanted and would have done. Step by step.

A Darkness Held

In God's wildness lies the hope of the world.
— John Muir

Imogene McCrary fingers her rosary and waits patiently while Father Seda mumbles a prayer for Sister Clement, whose legs are rigged in traction. It has been thirty-six hours since her fall down a metal staircase outside Saint Mary's Star of the Sea, and Father Seda has roped Imogene, a former student of Sister Clement's, into this visit.

When Father Seda finishes his prayer, Imogene makes as if to touch Sister Clement, but Sister Clement slaps her hand away hard. With a crooked finger, Father Seda lifts a slat of the blinds and winces at the daylight unfiltered and sharpened by the glass. Outside the traffic moves along the north Oregon coastal highway, all the logging trucks and campers and buses pushing into the wind. Everyone is just passing through Gearhart toward someplace else.

"We're all so sorry about that spill down the stairs. I hope you don't fault the children." Father Seda speaks to the glass, to the flat table of sea beyond the spit of land outside.

"I didn't fall. I was pushed," Sister Clement says through clenched teeth. Her voice shakes with fury or pain, Imogene can't tell which. She's too busy watching the transparent bag clipped to the bed rail soundlessly fill with urine. It's been over three years since Imogene has seen Sister Clement at mass, and now she's having a hard time getting used to this new image of the nun. Instead of her black woolen habit, Sister Clement is wearing a pale green hospital gown with immodest slits in the side. With her legs hiked unceremoniously in the air, she appears small and ordinary and diminished, not at all like the fierce woman of superhuman size and strength Imogene remembers from her days in school, a woman whose sense of Christian duty and firm grip on the ruler fractured knuckles and gave middling students like Imogene's brother, Frank, small ulcers.

"Just watch yourself around those kids." Sister Clement turns toward Imogene. "They're not right." A fleck of spittle clings to her lower lip. "And for God's sake, don't turn your back on them—not even for a second!"

The woman is a nun, a bride, Imogene reminds herself. The spotless bride of Christ.

Father Seda clasps his hands. "Oh, they can't be that bad!" He laughs. "Ha!"—the rigid bark of a boy forced to sit perfectly straight in the presence of a nun for too long. Imogene rises from her chair, grabs a hospital pamphlet warning against the dangers of deep-vein thrombosis, and follows Father Seda out the door and down the hall of St. Michael's. The shadows they cast are crisp and their tread is soundless over the shiny waxed floor. He holds open the heavy glass door for Imogene and points to the parish station wagon in the parking lot. "She loves these children, she really does. It's just the pain talking." He draws his breath through his teeth. "It could have been so much worse. At least she has her arms."

Imogene nods, makes a clucking sound, and rubs the spot on her hand that is already rising to a bruise.

• • •

It's a short drive from the hospital to Saint Mary's Star of the Sea, where the upper floors of the church serve as the dormitory and school for the boarders, all children in grades K–12. Behind the church is the playground, an uncovered parking lot of hard-packed gravel spray-painted with hopscotch squares. The gravel crunches and pops under the tires as the station wagon labors over the lot. It's high tide and the wind off the water a few blocks away sends the monkey bars clacking, the canary-yellow tetherball on the chain bobbing. The children, all fifty of them, are shrieking. Two girls shower a smaller, red-haired girl with gravel. The teacher's aide, Judy Johns, grimaces fiercely and wrings her hands. Imogene knows her from high school, and the few times Imogene attended mass she saw Judy there, lighting candles with Sister Clement. Judy's got jumpy nerves and a bad stomach, which is what the prayer candles were for, and Imogene knows that Judy won't try to intervene with the children.

Father Seda switches off the engine. Together they squint at the children. The light is like that here, sharp enough to force a grimace but never warm enough to cause a sweat.

"I know it's short notice, but we need a sub, and I heard you needed the work." Father Seda turns to Imogene. "Besides, Sister Clement asked for you specifically."

"Why me?" She is beyond bewildered. If anyone knows how unfit she is for a sub job these days, it's Sister Clement and Father Seda, who have recently spotted her leaving the AA meetings held in the basement of the church and heading directly to the bar across the street.

With his thumb Father Seda pushes his glasses higher on the bridge of his nose. "You're one of her old students. You'll remember how she wants her class run."

Imogene swallows. She remembers well her days in Sister Clement's classroom. She remembers Frank sitting at the desk in front of hers. It was Sister Clement's habit to assault Frank

with the catechism, a series of questions regarding man's purpose and relationship to God, while it was Frank's habit to
stand there trembling, a stream of urine speeding down his leg.
"Give me a day to think about it," Imogene says at last, shoving
open the door and sliding from the cracked seat.

Before she lost her teaching license on account of her drinking, when Imogene was still working in the Clatsop County
and North Plains sub pool, she'd get calls from schools as far
north as Astoria and as far south as Manzanita. And because of
the money, she'd go. Because of the money, she'd endure that
awful moment of stepping through the door of a classroom and
being sized up by the students. In Warrenton she could always
smell the contempt of the sixth-grade girls—sixth-graders!
—who already knew how to wear makeup and high heels,
whose slim hips rolled with the lazy walk of people who knew
things Imogene never would. Those were the days when she
wished for the refuge of a uniform as full as a habit. Growing
up poor and with a horsy face, Imogene had as a high school
student contemplated life in a convent, a life balanced between
service to others and solitude, a comfortable prospect. If nothing else, she could hide her bulging body behind the thick
folds of the habit, that floor-length costume that made even the
fat nuns look as if they floated on air when they walked.

As graduation approached and everyone else in her class,
Judy Johns included, settled on a mate or a job or more education, or all three, Imogene settled on nothing. And though
she had never been one for visions, one day the answer seemed
to present itself in this way as she was standing beside Sister
Clement. A shaft of light illuminated the nun's face and neck,
and she tipped her chin toward the sun. The lenses of her
glasses reflected such a piercing brightness that Imogene had to
shield her eyes. Feeling in her rudderless, girlish heart a roiling

mixture of fear of Sister Clement and terrible desire for her approval, Imogene decided right then that she would in fact be a nun, an Ursuline like Sister Clement, and Imogene made the mistake of saying so.

"Some girls aren't built for it. It's a lonely life," Sister Clement said, gripping the railing, and Imogene noticed for the first time how chapped her knuckles were, how red the meat of her fingers. "A nun never stops being a nun. We don't have off hours or breaks," she explained. "We can drink a little, but never, ever do we smoke." Sister Clement turned and gave her a thorough look. Imogene and her brother Frank were known for their halos of smoke and their trail of cigarette butts.

"I could quit smoking," Imogene said.

"You mean for Lent, like."

"No, for good."

Sister Clement snorted. "Too late. If God is the air we breathe, then our lungs must be pure." She poked Imogene in the chest with a finger. "I'll bet your pipes are so tarred you couldn't run up and down these steps without getting winded."

The steps were narrow and steep, and one look told Imogene that Sister Clement was right. The next day Imogene filled out loan applications for a series of teacher training courses at the community college, stopped talking about being a nun, and started drinking and smoking more.

Imogene lights another cigarette and steps out onto the cinderblock porch of her singlewide. Overhead the wind pushes the clouds to the horizon, where the sky is rare-steak red. The kind of sky the fishers and crabbers like, and if the water doesn't go to chop, she might soon see the lights of their boats. She inhales deeply, draws the smoke into her lungs, thinks she's burning, on fire, and smiles.

She's turning thirty-eight in two days. A time in a woman's

life when she looks in the mirror and asks herself questions she already has the answers to. A terrible age, she decides. Still, a woman makes her desperate gestures, and Imogene has followed the female prescriptive. *Shed a few pounds.* This she has done by climbing a used StairMaster. *Smile more.* This she is also working on. Last spring she bought lipstick, a first for her. For a few brief months she thought her plan for catching a man worth keeping was actually working: Mick from the garage asked her out to a movie, and she happily said yes.

Mick lasted three weeks. When she realized he would not be calling her again, there was some shame, a quick pang of guilt. Once again she'd failed to keep herself pure. Then came a sagging relief, that flimsy hanky good for when the sure and swift realization hit: she'd been dumped. Again. Out went the StairMaster, out onto the crushed razor-shell drive.

After Mick came Glen from Rexall's. Glen, for whom she'd tweezed her eyebrows, lasted less than a week. Shopping for lipstick or anything else at Rexall's was out of the question after he dumped her, and then she had to drive to Astoria to buy economy-sized bottles of aspirin and boxes of Franzia, a pink blush that came in a cardboard container equipped with a spigot. After Glen and a few others like him, Imogene began to think that there was nothing quite as reliable as a box of wine and the way it made her feel after she'd emptied it.

When she considers the reliable ingredients that make up her life—the misery of being routinely dumped, the comfort of boxed wine—she can't overlook her many sub jobs in the lower grades. And she suddenly feels generous. Children may give her a headache, but nothing seems as right or true. And though they may make demands, may disappoint, rarely do they break her heart. From her pocket Imogene retrieves a bottle of Digitek and taps out two pills, holds the bottle to her ear, and gives it a shake. Kids do not expect as much. You can screw up and they'll forgive you. At least the young ones are like that. For all these reasons and a few more, Imogene genuinely likes children more than she thought she would, and she gets pangs some days, wanting a few of her own. This is the clincher, the deciding vote. Imogene leans against the glass slider, gummy in the tracks with sand, then makes her way to the kitchenette to call Father Seda.

The entire room bursts with hands on Imogene's first day at Saint Mary's: orange palm prints bordering the wall are turkeys, the thumbs forming the heads and wattles. Green hands are shamrocks, blue prints are peacocks, purple ones fat starfish. Hands are the sun, the fingers the rays. Ten fists are ten moons. Ten fists pressed knuckle side down are owls perched on the thick branches of thumbs.

A weary fleet of ancient microscopes is stationed on the desks, and behind each microscope sits a third-grade child, staring at her, measuring her, reading the lines on her face. But they're too young, she decides, and too small to have pushed a nun as substantial as Sister Clement down a staircase.

Imogene clears her throat. "My name is Miss McCrary, or Miss M, if you like. I know we are all keeping Sister Clement in our prayers, and she wanted me to thank you and tell you that she misses you all." She can feel her smile going stale. It's sneaky to speak for someone else. But she's alone here, and she can feel her confidence quickly evaporating.

In the front row a boy lifts his fat, grimy hand high in the air. "You're not a nun, are you?" he asks. His hair is so blond it threatens an instant headache.

"No," Imogene says, fingering her white lace collar. The collar is attached to the most conservative blouse she owns, the closest she'll ever get to passing for a reformed nun, but even in this, she realizes, she has failed.

"I can tell because of your shoes. Sister Clement's don't make any noise on the floor," says a dark-skinned boy with a large bandage over his arm.

"And you don't have any kids either, do you?" a freckle-faced girl with thick glasses says, her hand trailing up into the air as an afterthought. In Imogene's day, such a tardy hand-raising would have earned this girl a whack from Sister Clement's ruler.

"No. But now I have all of you," Imogene says with a wink, so they will think of themselves as small gifts, the way she is reminding herself right now to think of them.

The children continue to stare. They don't even blink, Imogene notes as she lowers herself carefully into Sister Clement's chair and discovers the secret of the woman's mysterious height. Stashed at the back of the knee hole are rubber-soled platform shoes, and on the seat of the chair extra cushions. Imogene glances at the lesson book Sister Clement keeps for herself: five empty squares headed with five different subject titles. The first square is for science, a subject she flunked twice under Sister Clement's tutelage, and Imogene feels her heart sinking.

"Let's play a game." Her voice hits the far wall and bounces back. "I'll call out your name and you tell me one interesting science fact you've learned this week." Imogene runs her finger across the top of the roster. "Anders, David."

"When a horse is sick, it crosses its legs," says the blinding towhead in the front row. Beside his name Sister Clement has written a reminder to herself: *Introduce to hygiene.*

"Diegas, Rudy."

"A shark throws up its stomach once a month to clean it. Afterward it swallows it back down." Next to his name Sister Clement has written, *Sits in the back. Dark skin. Sneaky; watch him.*

"The universe has spots," says the girl named Graciella Fiero, her eyes trained on Imogene's throat. Graciella—the name is like water, and Imogene is surprised to see a big-chested girl stuffed into a too-small uniform raising a forearm over her head as if shielding herself from a blow. Imogene glances at Sister Clement's note: *Always a bruise on her arm. Pray for her; she probably needs it.*

"Not spots. Freckles," adds the red-haired Findlay girl. Sister Clement's note reads, *First name Eilis, pronounced A-lish. One of those weird Irish names.*

"A river has two sides, where it came from and where it is going." This from the tiny Morgan girl, whose voice melts like the pure notes of a bell. If Sister Clement has a favorite, she is probably it. Even though she's swimming in a starched blouse three sizes too large for her, she sits with perfect posture, her body like the letter *L* behind her desk. Imogene is not too surprised to see Sister Clement's comment: *Shows promise.* The closest the nun probably ever gets to doling out high praise.

Imogene closes the ledger. She bites her lip and tries to remember something, anything, from her teacher training classes that will help her fill up the remaining minutes of science hour. "Does anybody have any questions?" she asks, her voice as buoyant as she knows how to make it.

The Anders boy looks at the windows, and for the first time Imogene notices his funny-shaped head, dished in at the rear. She notices too that the windows, which had all been closed —she's sure of that—are open now and sand flies are buzzing into the room.

Lilly Morgan produces a multiplication worksheet and holds it aloft. "Do we have to fill in all these squares?"

The words bring an instant rush of gratitude. Yes, Lilly is the perfect student, rescuing a foundering sub. "Yes," Imogene improvises. "I'll collect them at the end of the hour." And the children bend over their worksheets, counting their fingers quietly against their desks and thighs, the sight so reassuring that Imogene thinks of saying a prayer of thanks as she pulls each of the windows closed and locks them one by one.

When the bell rings, the children file quietly through the door and merge with the other children in the school. They head down the hall to a door that leads to the metal steps. Imogene walks slowly beside them. No one speaks. But Catholic kids are like that, having been herded about all their lives with whistles and claps or, under Sister Clement's watch, a handheld clicker. One click from Sister Clement and the ordinary chaos of movement settled to a full stop, which Imogene knew signaled to Sister Clement perfection in parochial training. But Imogene has never believed in clicking or whistling. A child is not a dog, she thinks as she walks to the head of her small rank of students.

Imogene opens the door and the children push past her, jostling against her body, nearly lifting her off her feet. She grabs for the railing and thinks again of Sister Clement, her broken legs, the spittle on her lower lip, her rage. Imogene can see now how easily it happened—one misstep on a fatigued flight of stairs, or a well-laced shove to a hip. It probably never occurred to Sister Clement that such elemental fixtures in her routine—these stairs, her students—could ever fail her.

Imogene sits on the topmost step, pops a Digitek to settle her jittery heart, and lights a cigarette, determined to smoke her way toward inner calm and not to let her suspicions get the best of her. At the far edge of an overgrown field, where the dune grass and scotch broom grow tall and sharp, the older boys take turns lashing one another. It's an old game her brother Frank used to play, called crown of thorns. Whoever looks the most like Jesus, forehead scored and palms reddened, wins. The girls on the gravel lot don't play so much as huddle, and some of the younger girls play a game called faith. They stand on a raised log, cross their arms over their chests, close their eyes, and fall backward, trusting that the three girls standing behind will catch them. Mercy is a more active game that favors girls with long fingernails and strong wrists. Imogene watches two girls pressing the heels of their palms together and lacing their fingers. With a whip of their wrists, they roll their hands under. Imogene winces, remembering this game, the rows of crescent-shaped cuts on her own hands and the quick cries of *Mercy,* what you said when you couldn't stand the biting of the fingernails anymore.

"You shouldn't smoke." A high-pitched girl's voice floats up through the stairs. Imogene squints down at Lilly, standing below, the light leaking through the metal steps spotting her forehead and neck.

Imogene inhales deeply and blows the smoke out in a graceful arc. "Why do you say that?"

Lilly climbs the stairs slowly and stops when her eyes are level with Imogene's. "Smoking can kill you, you know."

The very words Imogene had said to Frank the first time he offered her a cigarette. Imogene leans and grinds her cigarette beneath her heel.

Lilly lowers her head and her stringy brown hair falls over her face. A shy slip of a girl, she reminds Imogene of a former version of herself standing there, chipping at the flaking scales of rust on the railing. A crow calls out and a dog answers. Then Lilly is gone. In her place is Judy Johns climbing the shaky stairs. She is a wiry woman with an exaggerated sense of devotion to all things Catholic. As a young girl, even before it was expected or required, Judy wore a bracelet studded with tiny charms of every saint she could find. And any time she passed the doorway of the chapel, even if it was just to go to the bathroom, Judy would stop short and genuflect, actually touching her forehead to the floor. Imogene suspects that it is this same frenzied sense of duty that year after year keeps her involved in the school and the parish without pay. Judy Johns gives guitar lessons, organizes bingo games, resides in the dorms, and oversees the care of the female boarders. And Imogene has to admire her for her tireless servitude. She is like Imogene, thirty-eight, a survivor of Sister Clement's class. Even worse, Judy has lost a husband at sea and a child, stillborn. Most women would have gone barking mad. But not Judy Johns, who possesses a persistence, a way to keep on keeping on, that both amazes and frightens Imogene.

Together they watch the fifth- and sixth-grade girls surround the Findlay girl, the only third-grader available. She tucks her chin to her chest and holds her arms at her sides as the other girls gather handfuls of crushed razor shells and gravel. The girls let loose with a volley of shells and rocks and the Findlay girl, mouth clamped, stands there taking it. Purgatory is the name of this game. If you duck, you have to stand there for double the time. If you keep your eyes open and ask for more, you are let go early.

"They're rough, all right, but you've got to love these games." Judy clicks her tongue, her gaze steady on the girl bearing up under heavy fire.

Imogene rubs the backs of her arms, remembering how she and Judy could stand there longer than anybody, until they were bleeding or Sister Clement's shrill whistle broke things up. Even then it was the conviction of the teaching staff that suffering was an essential component of good Catholic education and a basic prerequisite for any true character formation.

Imogene observes the Findlay girl. She doesn't even flinch! And though she's a small girl, she seems too old to be a third-grader, too composed. Especially given the nature of these games, which have, if anything, grown more vicious. The stones the girls throw are larger, the weeds longer, and Imogene soon wonders what it is about suffering that these kids are actually learning.

A bell rings and the children file up the steps and back into their respective classrooms. Imogene is just about to sit on Sister Clement's stacked chair when she sees that the windows have been thrown open again. The flies swoop into the room and buzz around the desk and the soured heel wells of Sister Clement's shoes. "Why are these windows open?" Imogene asks, but no one answers. She walks to the windows and, one by one, pulls them closed.

"It stinks in here," Lilly Morgan sings out. Then Graciella pinches her nose and Rudy, the boy in the back, does the same. Imogene notices that his wound has spread past both sides of his bandage. Imogene sniffs, thinks she can smell it.

And she notices again David's funny-shaped head and Lilly's eyes that are too big for her small face, and as Imogene backs into the blackboard, an oily sense that something is not right rises in her stomach. *Knock it off,* she chides herself, feeling silly and foolish for so quickly losing her composure. But as she straightens and distributes oversize pieces of white paper and boxes of crayons to the children, she can't help looking at their hands, their strong wrists, can't help wondering.

"We like drawing," David says, tapping his feet. "There aren't any test questions or quizzes, and we always draw the same thing."

Imogene blinks at his shock-white hair. In her day they drew what Sister Clement told them to. Lazarus' sloppy resurrection or Jesus' oozing heart if Easter was approaching. The thought that Sister Clement was loosening up in her later years, or at least letting them draw happier pictures, makes Imogene glad for the children; they will have fewer reasons to hate the woman later. But it saddens her to know that people do change in ways they can't help, even if it's for the better, and suddenly she feels sorry for Sister Clement.

"Maybe we could let Sister Clement know we miss her." Imogene's words tumble out as the ideas come upon her. "We could draw get-well pictures to cheer her up. And then tomorrow I can deliver them to her."

Rudy has already rolled his paper into a tight scroll and is swatting at a fly. But the other students stare intently at Imogene.

"What if she doesn't get well?" David picks at a scab on his knee.

"A picture can't help you get better," the Findlay girl says quietly, wrinkling her nose so that her freckles gather. Imogene looks at her, at those freckles spattered in dark confusion over her face, and suddenly thinks that she needs a drink, or three, maybe four.

For twenty minutes the children work in silence as Imogene makes the rounds. They pick their noses without shame. It's enough to make her smile, though she's careful about that. When she took the training courses, she was told to try to be inconspicuous, especially around the making of art. Being inconspicuous was not a technique employed by Sister Clement. But then, it would be hard, Imogene decides as she stands behind David, to be inconspicuous if you were the only ruler-wielding Ursuline nun still wearing a full habit when every other nun in the country had long ago adopted more casual dress.

In the center of his empty paper, David draws a black dot. He grinds the crayon in a tight circle, following the contour of the dot so that it grows into a three-dimensional layer of wax. At the desk next to his, Lilly draws an oval, the crayon squeaking over the wax with each pass. The Findlay girl (Imogene will never get that first name, she knows—no use trying) grips a black crayon and draws something larger, something with a hump or a head, an elephant or a camel. Imogene can't tell which, and rather than ask and embarrass both of them, she presses her lips together and moves on to Rudy's desk. His picture is a tangle of black scribbles.

Imogene can't help herself. "What's that supposed to be?"

"The dark middle. It moves real fast, see?" Rudy taps at the tangles.

"Nice," Imogene says, hoping that Rudy doesn't notice the too-bright tone of her voice.

Graciella is the real artist—even through the scrim of her hair hanging over her drawing, Imogene can detect an animal's bristled coat, teeth, claws.

"That's really wonderful." Imogene touches her elbow. Graciella winces, hunkers low.

"It's God. Wild." Graciella's voice frays to a whisper. "But good." She turns her drawing face down.

Imogene blinks and steps away. She stations a tape dispenser on an empty desk and observes the children, one by one, slipping to the back of the room to tape their drawings to the wall. When Imogene sees their pictures side by side, she has to sit down. They read like a series of animated panels, a sure story emerging from square to square. David's dot grows to Lilly's oval, which becomes the Findlay girl's animal with legs. Rudy's picture of darkness and the speed with which it flies through the air becomes Graciella's image of a dog, mouth open, eyes glinting, lunging beyond the boundaries of the white square and into the classroom.

Of course Sister Clement taught her class the same thing so many years ago, how a dot becomes a dog, how it pleases God, inscrutable in his ways, to assume such shapes so that we might better see and understand him. But the quickness of their hands, the sureness of their strokes shakes her up. Two minutes later, Imogene's heart is locked in a stutter and she can feel a ten-aspirin headache brewing. She knows she will spend the rest of the afternoon and evening in her trailer, emptying a box of Franzia.

What she can't tell anyone is that she's doing the world a favor when she drinks. The first drink relaxes the muscles in her jaw. The second keeps them relaxed. The third makes her benevolent, spacious in her heart and mind and lungs. Alcohol sands down her complicated grief for all things lost—her parents and Frank and even those things and people she has never had and dares not hope for. But on days like these, when she's increasingly long on recall, she thinks it isn't fair that her memory pains her the way it does. And this she can't quite understand: why God would make life hurt if it were meant to last so long. This, she decides, is further proof that God not only winks at a full-blown drinking problem but is actually egging her on.

But this kind of thinking only confirms what Imogene has suspected all along. Sister Clement had been right; Imogene would have been a terrible nun. Forget the fact that she has lost her teaching license on account of the drinking. Forget the fact that she was never the best of Sister Clement's students, was held back on account of her mind, which wandered, though it was hard to say where. She supposes it drifted to playground games. To shapes in the sky, muscled forms that made her think she could see faith and hope in the substantiality of cloud.

Half a pack of cigarettes and one third of the way through the box of Franzia, Graciella's words churn inside her: *Wild, but good.* It reminds her of something Sister Clement once said, all those years ago when Imogene was a third-grader, sitting perhaps in the very same seat as Graciella. Imogene never forgot it. Sister Clement had been teaching a poem called "The Hound of Heaven." That Imogene can remember the lesson, as drunk as she is, is a tribute to Sister Clement's matchless teaching technique: fear + shame + humiliation = total recall. Yes, Imogene got that poem memorized and can even remember with caustic clarity Sister Clement's explanation of the poem's meaning. God is a dog, untamed and wild, who comes, in his grace, to overtake us in spite of ourselves, to save us from ourselves when we don't even know we need it. Imogene remembers gripping the sides of her desk so hard that her hands cramped. These were terrible words corroborating everything she suspected about God: he was mean and toothy and long on punishment, just like Sister Clement. "It's a hard kind of grace, and might even hurt a little," Imogene remembers Sister Clement explaining.

"Why?" Imogene had asked, and Frank groaned quietly in the desk in front of Imogene's.

"Well, a dog does have teeth, doesn't it?" Imogene is sure she remembers a thin smile drifting across Sister Clement's face and just as quickly disappearing.

Frank's hand went up. "Is this going to be on a test?" And Sister Clement pressed her lips together tightly, the way she always did just before her ruler came whistling down.

Imogene pours another drink, four fingers. God may be wild, but good? She's not so sure. At this very moment she decides that tomorrow she'll look those kids straight in the eye and tell them a thing or two about the God she knows.

The phone jolts her. She senses before she answers that it will be Judy, out of breath, calling from the hospital. Sure enough, it is. "Imogene, it's Sister Clement," Judy rasps. "She's taken a turn and she's asked for you—specifically. Bless her, she's such a saint. So close to God, lying there, smiling."

"She's probably higher than a kite." Imogene squints at the clouds outside.

"She's a good woman. You shouldn't say things like that. She's had a hard life."

Haven't we all, Imogene wants to say. So what if Sister Clement joined up with the Ursulines by default, after almost being married and losing her fiancé just days before the wedding. It was an old joke with Frank: the man probably died at the thought of waking up beside her for the rest of his life. But nobody made her join, nobody made her teach children. Sister Clement chose those things for herself, and to this day Imogene can't imagine why. She downs the rest of her drink. "Frank wet the bed because of her," Imogene says to Judy at last, sliding the receiver back onto its cradle.

And after being turned down by the army on account of their family history of bad hearts, he enrolled in seminary to prove to people like Sister Clement that he was worth something. A year later, after he was dismissed from the Jesuit priesthood—a failure, ashamed—he climbed into his bathtub, cut his wrists along the leaders, and quietly died.

Banks of machines blinking and dripping and beeping transform Sister Clement's room into a metered cacophony. An oxygen tube snakes down her throat, and Father Seda explains to Imogene how a blood clot in Sister Clement's leg is threatening to break off at any moment and lodge in her lungs. Now the ordinary air in the room, being a mere 12 percent oxygen, is not enough for the woman. But even with the purer air, Imogene can see that Sister Clement is leaving them all behind; she is shrinking, and her hands, unmoored without a ruler or a clicker to hold, rove over the vast canvas of white bed sheet.

Imogene carefully sidesteps a brown paper bag that holds Sister Clement's habit, neatly folded. She nods hello to Judy. Only then does she notice the pictures tacked up around the room, the five pictures her students drew earlier that day of the black dot becoming a dog. At the bottom corners the children have pressed their signature palm prints.

Judy pats Sister Clement's hand, but the woman's gaze is locked on the drawings.

"Who hung these pictures up?" Imogene asks.

"Why, the children, of course." Judy looks at Father Seda, who looks at Sister Clement.

"They came here?" Imogene can hear alarm rising in her voice.

"And they recited a poem for her—you know, the one about the dog Sister Clement teaches every year during Lent."

"I remember it." Imogene swallows, tastes something bitter.

Judy approaches the drawings and stands just inches from the black crayon wax. "Those kids are really smart. They got that entire poem up by heart, every bit of it, without so much as a stumble or a stutter."

"It was incredible," Father Seda says softly.

"Well, suffer the children." Judy begins to recite scripture.

Imogene steps to Sister Clement, leans into her line of vision, and sees that her pupils are dilated, large black dots. They begin to water slightly, and she reaches for Imogene's hand. She grips her hand—pats it, even. Imogene blinks. It's the closest, she knows, the woman will ever get to expressing true affection. Sister Clement's brows suddenly join in a frown. She moves her head slightly and fixes her gaze again on the drawings. Imogene turns her head and studies the pictures, thinking that if she stares at them long enough, she will glimpse what it is that Sister Clement sees.

The walk home from the hospital takes Imogene past a long line of trailers, each of them ugly, but no two ugly in exactly the same way. As she passes the neighbors' property, their hound lifts his snout and bays. His voice rises and falls in the wind. It's the saddest, most baleful sound she's ever heard, and as she sidles past her abandoned StairMaster, the handles of which she now uses to hang her laundry, Imogene actually considers praying for the dog.

In her bedroom she can hear a slant rain beginning to fall, tapping the corrugated roof. She pours a tall glass of Jim Beam and considers Sister Clement. No one would accuse the woman of being beautiful, but neither can Imogene deny that there in the hospital room, with her face soft, her eyes wet and focused on those drawings, one hand on Imogene's, Sister Clement became lovely in a way that defied explanation. Gone was her trademark rage and bitterness, and in its place was something almost like calm, or even tenderness. It was a sight so unfamiliar that Imogene still doesn't quite know what to think.

The phone rings.

"It's Sister Clement," Father Seda says, his voice thin and spectral. "She's gone on. We'll say prayers for her at the church tomorrow afternoon and hold a memorial mass this Saturday. Do you want me to tell the children?"

"No," Imogene says after a long pause. "I'll do it."

With the rain teletyping messages on her roof and the neighbors' hound yodeling, it's a long time before Imogene can sleep. Her thoughts are roiling. And while she hoped she might drink her way toward an epiphany, it's clear to her now the bottle is empty that she's just as bewildered as ever. It's not that she ever thought any of them were invincible. Frank was built of timid constitution and too good for this world anyway. But a woman like Sister Clement was far too sturdy to die the way she did, and Imogene thinks again of the children, taking it upon themselves to visit the woman. What did they tell her, she wonders, when they bent over her bed to offer their comfort? What else do they know about that they've not told Imogene?

· · ·

She takes her time getting to school the next morning. The wind off the water blasts so fiercely that it drives the tears from her eyes across her temples and into her hair. She is surprised by her sorrow. She is astonished to discover that she will actually miss Sister Clement, whom she has somehow learned to appreciate, as one appreciates the growling of an old generator. The noise and fury just become so familiar over time that they actually bring comfort. After all, Sister Clement is—was—one of the few people left who remembered her and Frank as children, and without her, Imogene feels suddenly very alone.

When she gets to the school, she smokes three cigarettes before she feels bucked up enough for the classroom.

Graciella is the first to stop by Sister Clement's desk. "Do you know what happens to you when you die?" she asks Imogene.

The question sounds odd, considering the grim message Imogene has to give the class. "You don't have to be afraid of that," she says. The wound on Graciella's elbow is darker, and Imogene stifles the urge to touch the girl.

"I know." Graciella's gaze settles on Imogene's open purse and her near-empty vial of heart meds. "But I'm worried for you."

The bell rings and Graciella drifts back to her desk, where she huddles with David, Rudy, and the Findlay girl, their gazes trained on Imogene. The flies loop in lazy arcs through the windows, and Imogene doesn't even bother closing them. Instead she faces the children, takes a breath,

"I have sad news, class. Sister Clement has passed away."

The children look at her calmly, completely unsurprised. David rubs the back of his funny-shaped head.

Imogene swallows. "That means we won't see her here, but someday we'll see her in heaven."

"Is this going to be on a test?" Rudy asks. "Because that's not an essential mystery, and today is Wednesday, and we always talk about essential mysteries on Wednesdays." He scratches at his scab.

Imogene frantically thumbs through the book of lesson plans. Silly, she knows, because they are as blank and open as a wide-brimmed day. Except for that fuzzy notion that God might be a dog, she can't remember the essential mysteries, and realizes that perhaps she never knew them in the first place. Again she wishes she had been a better student, or at least had had the foresight to bring another pack of cigarettes today. "OK," she says at last. "You call out the essential mysteries, and I'll list them on the board."

"Bread is life. That's why you aren't supposed to cut it with a knife." This from Lilly in a singsong patter, and Imogene struggles to keep up at the board. The flies are starting to get to her. And her lungs ache a little, and she realizes she shouldn't have had that last cigarette.

Then Rudy, swatting flies in the back of the room, says, "A guitar is fitted with its own coffin. So are a turtle, a violin, and a pair of shoes."

"Sacrifice comes from shelter," Graciella says, her finger trailing an entry in an enormous dictionary balanced on her knees. "That's why those on the threshold need the biggest push."

David, sitting beside Graciella, flips through the pages and taps a dirty finger in the margin beside another entry. "Danger comes from the Lord."

"A blessing is a thrashing at a wound." The Findlay girl adjusts her glasses. "That's why scar tissue has to be broken to be beaten."

Imogene squints at the girl, fighting hard to focus.

The buzzing in her ears and in the classroom begins to echo. Fresh air, she thinks, will clear her head. Imogene drifts to the open windows. Outside, the hard-packed gravel is gray and wet, the weeds sharp and glinting. The fog lowers and the sky flattens. In a blink everything clarifies to its elements: the sky becomes water and salt. She feels the salt grainy on her face, and she thinks of Sister Clement's face transformed. Thinks of revisions, remedies, and unexpected gentleness. She thinks of teeth.

The Findlay girl slides out of her chair and stands beside Imogene. She nods at the open windows. "Are you afraid?" she asks.

Before Imogene can answer, Rudy and Graciella pipe up. "Sister Clement told us that just because a dog has teeth doesn't mean it will bite."

"What?" Imogene asks. In her own ears her voice sounds foreign and astonished.

"Because it pleases him sometimes to assume such shapes." Lilly's voice sails across the room, though her head is bent over her paper and she's drawing frantically.

Except for the Findlay girl, they are all drawing on oversize sheets of paper, black crayons gripped in their hands. Graciella is scoring the sleek lines of a large hound, and next to her Rudy presses his crayon so hard that the paper threatens to tear.

All right, Imogene sighs, relieved and then surprised that at a moment like this she can feel relief. It's just one more thing on a long list of things she has miscalculated. Well, she'll stay right here, right by the windows where she's supposed to be. Stay for as long as she needs to, for as long as these children need her.

Air as pure as gin rises up from the ground beneath the windows. The Findlay girl gives Imogene's hand a quick squeeze and Imogene leans forward, pushes open the windows as wide as the hinges will allow.

The Hurler

ON CLOUDLESS DAYS, I love to watch the smooth flights of couches and tables. Dead animals are good too, their feet and tails, wings and fins stiff and unbending as they clip the top of my laurel hedge, their bodies sailing into the abandoned dump on the other side of my fence. It's beautiful in the sense that getting rid of the trash can be beautiful and satisfying. There's a freedom in tripping that release, in watching broken and abused objects sail through the air, in that moment when the sprocket-driven winch tightens the slack and *whoosh,* something unbearably cumbersome takes one last ungainly flight and lands in the soft litter of potato peelings, bicycle parts, and motor oil.

The hurler started small, as a hobby. When my parents died, it was my job as their only child to empty their house. I looked around the cluttered living room, at the old bellflower-shaped gramophone that breathed the fragrance of moths, at the volumes of ornamental books with gold-embossed spines. I noticed Ferdinand, my father's hedgehog, now stuffed, who'd quilled me many times when I was a girl for no good reason. But Dad loved that grumpy animal, and Mom did too. She cooked special meals for him, concocted herbal remedies when he sniffed or coughed suspiciously, cared for him as if he were another, better child. When I spied him in his old familiar pose, staring at me with his hard yellow eyes, those spines standing at attention, I knew where to start.

That night I began construction of my hurler, consulting my old high school physics textbook to make sure I understood the principles of counterweight and tension. I had never been good with numbers, had failed physics twice, and just this once I wanted to build something that worked. By morning I had finished, and I rolled my creation from the garage to the back yard. I placed Ferdinand on the old bicycle seat that served as the launch platform. In all my excitement, a few quills from his backside had fallen out, and I thought I should reattach them, maybe even say a little prayer for him. It was something my mother, a woman who couldn't be cruel even if she tried, would have done, maybe would have wanted me to do. But then I remembered how certain animals, cantankerous in life, could become even more so in death: snapping turtles that managed a final chomp, jellyfish trembling on the shore, anxious to get in that last sting. I didn't want to take any chances.

"Sorry, Ferdinand," I said, cranking the cable taut, each delicious click sending a shiver down my spine. I waited for a moment, basking in the heavy pause, my hand on the trip. I sprang the lever, and Ferdinand sailed high into the air, where the wind caught at his quills. For a brief moment, just before he plummeted into the motor oil moat surrounding the dump, he looked like he was flying.

I ran back to the house and hauled out the rest of my parents' clutter: their first, second, and third attempts at pottery and sculpture, their old cameras, all those self-help books about marriage. After I made a clean sweep of the ordinary household detritus, I rounded up neighborhood debris: a flattened opossum, a bird with a broken wing, an array of tires and burned-out hair dryers that had been tossed along a roadside ditch.

Three weeks of this went by. I thought I would get bored with my invention, at least tired of the novelty. But I didn't. Just the opposite. Each launch buoyed my spirits until I was giddy with joy and anxious to find more junk. I remembered my father's bagpipes stashed in the attic, a reckless and drunken purchase he'd made after watching the *Highlander* trilogy. I fought with the pipes all the way down the stairs and out to the hurler, as they hummed and wheezed in protest. I removed the bicycle seat launch pad and attached a pallet I'd designed for heavy, awkward items. I sprang the release, and the bags, still harboring some of my father's air, gave a final undignified squeak.

Just then Simon, my best friend since kindergarten and our neighbor from across the street, showed up, in time to hear the strangled landing of the pipes. Simon was my first kiss and reminded me of a more innocent time. Since then there had been nothing but bad luck for each of us in the love department, and I couldn't decide who was more miserable, me as I lived alone in my parents' house or Simon, who lived with his elderly mother. He whistled and opened a can of beer. Then he hopped up onto the pallet and bounced it up and down.

"What's the weight limit on this?"

I shrugged.

"You patent it yet?"

"I hadn't thought that far ahead."

Simon hopped off the hurler and left the yard, but I got to thinking. Why not let others loft their burdens and experience the same thrill I had been keeping to myself? And why shouldn't I benefit from it? That afternoon I placed an ad in the classifieds: "Hurler for hire. Cast your cares into nearby lot. No load too heavy. Rates reasonable." By the next evening a throng of people and their trash filled my yard. There was the widow from two blocks over with her husband's gold-handled golf clubs, and a crowd of jilted girlfriends and boyfriends, paying a dollar per launch to loft the fallout of their ruined romances: promise rings and ticket stubs tied in small bundles and weighted with bricks, bad birthday presents, ID bracelets, framed pictures of the formerly loved. But most often they brought their hearts, some empty, some broken. The saddest cases were the too-full hearts, the overworked ones still carrying good intentions and bad and all the fallout from a lifetime of lousy choices they'd promised themselves they'd forget but couldn't because they were too busy twelve-stepping their way through therapy.

Cracked and split at the chambers' seams, these hearts still managed to continue beating. I couldn't blame their former owners for jettisoning them. What good is a heart so wounded, rusted, stupid in its ways? What good this muscle that flexes only to prolong the pain? They were the tricky loads, these hearts, messy and dripping, and sometimes the owners weren't quite ready to part with them. "You're better off without it," I'd whisper, hoping my optimism came through.

The day after I opened for business, a girl showed up in my back yard, holding her heart in her hands. She looked like every other abandoned lover, nondescript in her devastation, red-eyed, her lips trembling. And then, of course, there was her heart: jagged and raw at the edges, beating unevenly. She approached the hurler and stood there biting her lower lip.

She looked so much like me, minus a few years, it hurt to see her. "You're doing the right thing," I said, wiping the pallet clean and snapping on my surgical gloves.

"I guess so," she said, sliding her heavy heart into my hands.

I let her trip the release for free and noticed with satisfaction that as she walked toward the gate, she had a lightness to her step that hadn't been there before.

At dusk, as I locked up the gate of my tired back yard with its trodden grass, I thought about those hearts throbbing away on the other side of the hedge. Then I went inside and lay down on the old bed from my childhood, looked out the window, and counted the stars until I fell asleep. That's when I dreamed of dead birds and fish creeping through the moat of motor oil that surrounded the dump and picking through the shrubbery (as if I couldn't hear them), crawling on their stiff little bellies, pushing through the dirt with their broken wings and fins, dropping feathers and flaking scales all the way. And then I dreamed the hearts unionized, got ideas, slithered over the dirt and through the hedge, an inch at a time, and made demands of me. I could hear them: *We are real. We are a part of you. You cannot do this to us.* But I wouldn't be taken in. I'd pull on my hip-waders if I had to, crawl under the hedge and push them back down with the garden rake, tell them to behave, remind them what they were: castoffs, second-stringers, damaged goods, the kind of hearts people were better off without.

A few days after I helped launch a neighborhood full of burden, Simon showed up again in my back yard, carrying a burlap sack over his shoulder, fireman style. The sack kicked, and from inside the burlap I could hear Mrs. Kreplachsky, Simon's mother, cursing her son.

I stuffed my hands into my pockets. "I can't launch your mother."

"Why not?" Simon loaded her onto the launch, though to her credit, Mrs. K. put up quite a fight, kicking with her little bird legs. An uneven load spelled trouble, I knew. With all her wiggling, I could see her winding up in the dogwood, wrapped around the lower limbs.

"Can you really call this living?"

I thought about Mrs. K., her yellow-brown eyes, her hard

and pointed anger. I recalled her habitual use of sarcasm as a means of educating Simon in the hurtful ways of the world. Every word she used was a jab, and I had learned years ago that the best line of defense was to show her a little cruelty, as that was the only thing she understood.

Just then Mrs. K. worked her way out of the sack and pulled the gag from her mouth, no easy feat.

"Listen you two little good-for-nothing, fart-head, jobless, lazy-ass—"

I helped Simon reinsert the gag, just missing Mrs. K.'s incisors, and said to Simon, "OK, I'll do it. But it'll cost you extra."

He pulled some bills out of his wallet and pressed them into my hand, then cranked the handle, all while his mother cursed from deep in her throat. With a loud snap, the hurler sent Mrs. K. flying, her toes grazing the hedge. Simon stood at attention, his hand at his forehead in a salute, until he heard his mother land on the other side. He kissed me on the cheek, quickly, then slid a can of beer into my hand and left.

I suddenly doubted my invention. It seemed ugly, a perversion of my truest intention: to initiate flight and weightlessness in both the hurler and the hurlee. After all, gravity always won the jackpot, holding us down until at last we submitted to the crush and were lowered to a final rest. I'd felt that I'd been doing a good thing by bringing smiles to all these people. But no longer, not with Mrs. K. so unceremoniously dispatched beyond the motor oil moat.

All that night and into the morning I heard Mrs. K. cursing her son, me, the hurler, the soupy moat full of bleeding, thumping hearts, which she claimed were giving her a pounding headache. She begged me to hurl over some melatonin for her insomnia. I launched it over to her with incredible accuracy, considering it was three in the morning. Still, knowing that she was out there lying in the waste of the neighborhood put a bad taste in my mouth. But I shouldn't have worried—the next morning Mrs. K. came crawling through the laurel hedge, her eyes amber and glassy like Ferdinand's. I jumped off my lawn chair and made a motion to help her.

She slapped my hand, moving from her elbow. "I never liked you," she said, and negotiated through the piles of trash yet to be hurled. She headed back to her own house, where I knew there'd only be more noise and another sleepless night.

Now Simon has taken a lesson from me, he says, and has set up shop in the basement of his mother's house: RETRIEVAL FOR HIRE.

"You know, for all those people who, for whatever reason, want their crap back," he explained last night as I was locking up.

I nodded. Overhead was an oilstone sky, and I wanted to clean the hurler before dark. "That's great," I said. It seemed like the perfect career for Simon. As his mother's caretaker, he'd become a shrewd observer of human regret. Surely there'd be misgivings, some longing among those who'd lofted their trinkets, all those forlorn reminders and fatigued hearts.

Behind us, I could hear Mrs. K. shrieking in her kitchen. Six o'clock and she was burning their dinner, blaming the pots and pans for it, from the sound of the beating she was giving them.

"Later," Simon said, with a lift of his hand.

"OK," I said, shutting the gate. I grabbed my bottle of super solvent and headed for the hurler. It occurred to me then that in addition to having an enterprising imagination, Simon had a mean streak, as was evidenced by his wanting to hurl his mother, whether she was ready to go or not. Clearly his mother was no treat, but his actions bothered me. It bothered me even more that this was what we had in common: our jaded, mean-spirited hearts.

I knew what I had to do. With exquisite clarity, I saw for once where my real trouble lay: not with my father's wheezing pipes or Ferdinand's needles, but with me. I nearly laughed aloud. Almost everyone else had figured it out: the widow who launched her husband's golf clubs, the trembling girl who in a courageous act lofted her heart, which would only betray her again and again.

I placed my palm over my sternum and pressed until I could feel my heart. I took a deep breath, stuck my fingers down my throat, and removed it, as neat as you please, and placed it on the hurler. It wasn't broken, not badly, or terribly wounded —no more so than the average thirty-something-year-old woman's heart. Oh sure, it put up some token resistance. I began to remember the great fun we'd had, the joy of my record-breaking mile run during my junior year in high school, my one and only date with a boy from my biology class. My heart even bled a little on the plastic bicycle seat. I'll admit, I was moved, even thought about shoving the whole mess back inside my chest. But my heart had never been my favorite organ, had in fact shamed and compromised me many times by encouraging false hopes, inspiring hazy, nostalgic longings, and delivering grim prognostications of a future marked by loneliness. My lungs and kidneys, gloriously silent, had never tormented me like this.

"I'm sorry," I whispered. "I really am." I took a big breath, held it, then tripped the release. No longer feeling reluctant, I watched my heart sail and heard it land with a soft plop on the pulsing mound of other discarded hearts.

I pressed on my sternum again, feeling none the worse for wear, feeling in fact better, lighter in my chest, certain that I was breathing with a new expansiveness, able now to see with a new clarity, never so glad to be emptied and undone, without a pulse, without a plan.

From the Fourth Row

FOR FIVE YEARS NOW I've been illustrating advertisements
for a marketing firm. So far it has brought me ineffable joy and
an absurd degree of woe. Knowing this, Arnos, a friend from
my youth and my boss, asks me why I don't quit. But I tell him
to forget it—what is life but suffering, and what better in that
case than to suffer at the throne of the muse? The whole idea
brings water to my eyes, and I clutch my chest. Then Arnos
asks me if I've been drinking. This is our morning ritual, and
I've discovered these last five years that ritual, be it putting the
kettle on the stove or simply maintaining the habit of breathing, is as important as life itself, for it's ritual and nothing else
that gets you through.

Take Arnos. He sits in the largest desk at the front of the office, where the windows overlook Prague's famous astronomi-
cal clock in Old Town Square. At noon when the bells chime,
Arnos leans out the window to watch the Apostles whirl along
the circular track and ring out the hours. Then he races around
the office and resynchronizes all the clocks. I sit four rows
back, away from the wonder of that clock-shaped circus. The
desk closest to Arnos's and farthest from mine belongs to
Lanka, for whom I'm nursing a four-and-a-half-year crush.

She's got long auburn hair and dark Turkish eyes and has developed a firm and distinct habit of ignoring me. Asking her out would be possible, even routine, for some men, but not for me. I have small hands and small teeth. I feel a little embarrassed, even ashamed of these things, and I try to hide them as best as I can. I keep my hands in my pockets as much as possible, and I've grown a mustache. I try not to smile, and when I talk, I pull my lips over my teeth. But at night my jaw aches, and in the morning I have to do exercises to loosen my facial muscles. And, of course, I sit so far back, in the fourth row.

I work in New Accounts and I draw and paint advertisements featuring new products for would-be clients. These days we've got a lot of foreign investors in Prague, and nobody, not even Arnos, knows for certain who actually owns the company. Marek, who sits in the second row and who has a dyspeptic temperament, thinks it must be Europeans, because Arnos gets to take the entire months of July and August for holiday. It's a very continental policy, and Marek assures me it would never happen with Americans at the helm. Well, good health to Arnos, I say. I hope he goes to one of those renovated Komsomol camps, drinks cheap Armenian wine, and, with any luck, woos an aging schoolteacher into bed. Certainly he needs it. Just behind his left ear, in his otherwise dark hair, Arnos has a small swatch of hair that is bleached of all color. When we were only seven or eight—best friends even then—I scared him, on a lark. A little trail of red paint from the corners of my mouth and dribbling out of my ear and down my neck—that was all. But one look at me and Arnos fainted. The next day at school, as I sat behind him (for even then Arnos was ahead of me), I noticed a strange patch bled of its pigment. It seemed extraordinary that something so small, so stupid, had left an indelible mark and that it was me, someone so insignificant, who had caused it.

But in spite of everything, we're friends. After all, Arnos arranged the transfer from my old job—painting the men's lavs in various metro stations. And just in time, too. A man can only withstand paint fumes in closed-in spaces for so long. "I believe in you absolutely," Arnos said to me that day, with a mock punch to my shoulder. And I looked at the little white patch behind his left ear and thought, no matter what, I would not let him down.

But I've been noticing lately that my sketches simply won't cooperate. Sometimes my ideas defy me and fail to translate to concrete images. And sometimes it's something more serious. Today, for instance, Arnos assigned me to a new account— some western pharmaceutical company catering to American ex-pats who drink too much and don't like how they feel afterward. The company made a painkiller, Hair of the Dog, designed to counteract the ill effects of a hangover. I drafted mockup sketches for hours, beginning to feel as if I myself were hung over, as I am so often these days. That's when I had a flash.

Novak, in the second row, likes to pray a lot before he begins a sketch, and Dubcek puts on his earphones and listens to Johnny Cash. Then there's Marek, who keeps secondhand chairs nearby so that if he gets frustrated, he can smash them to bits against the urinals in the men's lav. Me, I like to rub my hands together, as if by doing so I might spark a fire. Then I pick up my pencils.

Today I drew a long-haired dachshund with a cold compress on his head and sunglasses over his eyes. Then I drew his big floppy ears standing up in straight lines, as if nothing, not even the grinding crush of gravity or a thumping headache, could keep this dog from partying. I painted the dog in oils, in mellow sepia browns and samovar gold, all the happy colors of fur. But by the end of the day, when I sat at my desk and looked at my painting, the dog's eyes had grown red and his ears were flagging. He looked as if he were suffering, as everything in this city has suffered. I stopped and studied him. The oils blurred at the edges of his body. I dabbed at the paint with a tissue, the whole time thinking that this was some elaborately con-structed joke, that Arnos or—dear God, please—Lanka would swing around the banks of easels, smile brightly, and tell me he or she had messed with my canvas while I was out for a smoke.

Five minutes passed. Blood pounded in my ears, the sound like that of a stick beating on a box. Then ten minutes. I asked Arnos if anyone had tampered with my canvas, and his eye-brows jumped the same way they did the one and only time I asked him for a raise. After twenty minutes of nobody own-ing up to anything, I reached into my desk for my cigarettes. We're supposed to go outside to smoke, especially now that Arnos has developed allergies and discovered his own mortal-ity. But smoking clears my head, so I lit a cigarette, propped my elbow on my desk, and considered my situation. I had to de-cide whether or not I was going to keep this business with the dog to myself. Out of the corner of my eye I could see the tail of the dog wilting, the cold compress sliding down his snout, knocking off his sunglasses. The whole mess was giving me a five-alarm cluster headache.

Finally I hid the painting behind my color boards and reached into the back of my tackle box of paints. I found the Hair of the Dog sample packets that the representatives had given us and swallowed them on my way to the lift.

I live in my mother's flat, in a building that has a big red hat painted on one side. It's an advertisement for toupees, and every time I see it I run my hand through my own thinning hair. Before I climbed the stairs, I stopped to deliver my rent to Manager Koza. Every month I suggest that he let me paint the other side of the building for him—a jazzy Energizer bunny, or maybe even one of my own designs. It's our ritual, Koza peering at me, his door opening just wide enough for me to slide my payment through and for him to hear me ask if I can paint the building. On this afternoon it was the same story. Koza asked from behind the door, "Are you famous, yet, Jiri B-Boura?" He pinched my check between his forefinger and thumb as if it were an asp.

"Not yet," I answered.

"Forget it, then," he said, and pulled the door closed.

I stomped up the stairs to my flat, where I sat by the window and made a point of drinking until I couldn't feel my head anymore—the last of my daily rituals. Before she died, my mama lived with me in this apartment building. Every day she'd sit by the window with Pepik, her stuffed canary, balanced carefully on her shoulder. Pepik had once had a brilliant life of sliced apples and small flights through the rooms and even the corridor, when Manager Koza was away. Pepik was prone to eye infections. Then he developed a cough, and he gave up the ghost one Easter morning. Mama took it as a propitious sign and had Pepik stuffed straight away. With his new clear eyes of glass, he never looked better, but then Mama started to decline. Though I whistled the songs of a canary to nourish her nostalgia, she grew listless and took to eating the last of Pepik's birdseed, crunching the tiny granules between her rotting molars as she watched the trains outside our building jerk and glide from Holesovice station toward the wet meadows behind the soot and noise of the city.

During her last days, her only pleasure was sitting at the window with Pepik on her shoulder. She'd watch the trains, mumbling about how well they kept to the schedules she'd hung on the wall next to the window. I thought it strange that she should acquire such an interest, for it was at that very station that every one of her family members had been loaded onto trains and transported to Terezin, where they were separated and, except for Mama, killed. Whether burned to death at Majdanek or gassed at Auschwitz she never said, and I never asked. All she had to say on the matter was that the heavens were cold and the humans living beneath it colder still. But the hoots and grumbles of trains made her happy, made her forget, and I encouraged her hobby in any way I could. I brought in tapes I'd made at a pet store, of turtledoves and the warm noises they made. Listening to the recorded birds, some of them remarkably Pepik-like in their squawks, and watching the trains beyond the window, Mama seemed happy enough. Then one day she began mistaking the Praha Express for the Night Train, the Vienna Special for the Brno–Budapest, and that's when I knew she wouldn't be with me much longer.

After Mama died, I found myself unable to escape the pull of the window. Through the glass I could see the trains heading out to warmer and brighter places. I'd sit there watching the night sky deepen to stars. It calmed me to know that there were thousands just like me in Prague, sitting at windows, wondering about all the others at their windows who watched for birds and people and trains. They were like me, I was sure —young, but old enough to have started to live, sitting at our windows, sipping cheap vodka, and telling ourselves that in those dark reflections of the panes we were not glimpsing our future.

When I woke up the next morning, I decided to go to the office early, put my troubles with Hair of the Dog behind me, and start working on something else. Arnos had assigned me two new projects: the Headwater Homes account, which would feature prototype apartments and cottages located upriver for people who could afford a view of water, and the

Copy General account, a retail photocopy/fax company. They were the biggest projects Arnos had ever given me and the ones, I was sure, that would bring me acclaim and take me a little closer to Lanka.

I sat at my desk, paper cups of coffee lining the edge. I blew on my hands, rubbed them together, and began sketching the homes, the expensive kind that sit just beyond the grit and the anger of the city, the kind that everyone talks about having. For kicks I penciled in a family: an older gentleman with a cane, whom I privately named Vaclav, and an older woman whose mouth folded into her face and who looked an awful lot like my mama. Last I drew a pouty woman in her twenties with a full chest and curvy hips. Good bone structure. Distance between the eyes good. A star-shaped face with the trademark strong Czech jaw. Long legs, very, very good. It occurred to me that I may have drawn Lanka, but in my head I nicknamed the woman Nika. I drew her holding a wire birdcage with a cheery yellow canary in it, and sitting on its haunches next to her a big, shaggy white dog.

But as soon as I was done with them, these people turned rebellious. Even as I drew them they wouldn't stay put, and pretty soon I had a shaggy dog and grandfolks and a canary and a curvy woman migrating from one frame to the next with complete disregard for where I had so carefully placed them. From their new stucco suburban flat with all the modern conveniences—gas heat, a refrigerator, and even an oven—the happy little family I had drawn picked up and moved to a house, a little brick cottage two frames over.

"Good God!" I sputtered, reaching into my top drawer for another Hair of the Dog sample. New Guy from the third row squinted in my direction. I hunched my shoulders and started redrawing the family, positioning them back in the flat and seated in front of a little color TV/radio, with wide smiles on their faces. As I got them settled in, Nika lit a cigarette. Then she started talking to me. "Leave us alone," she said with a toss of her auburn hair.

Four rows away I heard one of Arnos's colossal sneezes.

"Hold still!" I hissed at her. New Guy turned and arranged his face into a tight frown.

"Mind your own business," she returned, giving me the finger.

I decided I was either going mad or getting sick. With my thumbs, I felt for the glands in my neck, but the slippery devils slid away under the pressure of my fingers.

Arnos came up behind my desk and scratched the hair at the back of his neck. "Do you smell something, Jiri?" He leaned over my chair and wrinkled his nose.

"I can't go on like this!" I said, tossing my pencil into the open tackle box.

"What are you talking about?" Arnos rocked forward onto the balls of his feet, then back to his heels. Forward and back.

"My sketches are in an uproar," I blurted out.

"Oh." Arnos glanced at my sketch, at my family standing still as if frozen. "Well, get yourself together, then," he said. He disappeared, and I slid a blank board over my drawings, snapped the hasp of my tackle box, and called it a day.

The next day I woke up before the birds. I lay in bed thinking about my sketches and wondering whether anyone besides me had seen, heard, or smelled them. It seemed odd that such a peculiar problem should visit me alone, and yet when I considered my life, punctuated by a long string of disappointments — my dropping out of art school, my jagged little teeth, my inability to find a girl who can tolerate me for five minutes — I realized that an uncooperative sketch was a comparatively small blip on the dark screen of my failures. But then I got to thinking. If this problem were to continue, if it were to spread to every sketch I touched, well, then I'd be in for a lot of trouble. I bolted out of bed and pulled on my trousers. It was still early, and the trams and buses weren't running yet. Through the Strahov monastery and down Petrin Hill I walked. As I passed the orchards, the trees heavy with fruit and the scent of limes in the air, my heart dropped a notch or two in my chest and I felt my blood moving differently in my veins.

I arrived at the office an hour before anyone else. My sketches were exactly as I had left them the day before. I lined up a row of coffee cups along the edge of my desk and was just sharpening my pencils when Arnos materialized behind me, scratching at that white patch of hair. I began to wonder if he regretted giving me such a big account, and I remembered my decision that no matter what, I would not cause his heart to stumble or his body to faint.

"Have you gone mad?" Arnos grabbed a cup of coffee from me and set it on New Guy's desk. "Don't you know that all that coffee is bad for you? All the doctors are saying so."

"I don't care," I said, and really I didn't. If my heart galloped and raced and dropped at the finish line ahead of schedule, that was all right with me. But there are limits to what you can say, even to your best friend.

"How many cups do you drink in a day?" Arnos asked.

I took a quick inventory of my desk. "Six or seven. Eight. Maybe nine." I stopped and lit a cigarette and picked up another cup.

Arnos slapped his forehead with an open palm. "That's terrible, Jiri." He grabbed the coffee from me, took my cigarette, dropped it into the cup, and placed the cup upright in the bottom of my rubbish bin.

"Coffee is good for you," I said. I bent, fished the cigarette out of the cup, and took a big sip. "Just ask Svejk." I nodded toward my new Copy General design.

For over three years Copy General had been relying on its image of Good Soldier Svejk, standing at attention with his trademark goofy grin. Now they wanted a more artistic presentation of the Good Soldier, something contemporary. So I had drawn a tall, angular soldier standing in the shape of a Roman numeral one, which gave old Svejk a kind of superhero appearance. Then I had erased that silly smile from his face and drawn his hand at his forehead in a flying salute.

Arnos took one look and groaned.

"What's wrong?" I asked.

"Can't you keep the old Svejk and just change the border or the lettering?"

"The old Svejk looks like a drunk."

"But he's a national symbol," Arnos objected.

"No one even remembers who he is anymore. Besides, Copy General needs something brisker. Sharp and intrepid." From her perch in the first row, I could see Lanka watching us, her eyes inscrutable—with suspicion? Amusement? Who could tell?

A little later, after more coffee, I had a flash. I remembered my walk through the orchards and down the hill and how suddenly alive I had felt. It couldn't be for nothing, that feeling. I decided then that today would be the day when I took my hands out of my pockets and asked the beautiful Lanka for a date.

I walked past the third row, past New Guy, whose eyes swept over my shoes, my trousers, my mustache. I passed the second row, where Novak sat praying over a doomed sketch and Marek, red in the face, kicked at an extra chair, and I approached the first row, all fear and trembling. Lanka was chatting with a blond woman two desks over, and when the blondinka saw me, she brought her hand to her mouth and giggled. Lanka turned to me.

"Would you like to have coffee with me sometime?" I

cracked my knuckles one by one, wishing I could trade in 10 percent of my talent for 10 percent more charm.

"Coffee?" Lanka's eyes widened.

"Yes," I said, remembering to smile while keeping my teeth covered.

"I'd love coffee. Thank you very much." She dug into her purse and pressed some coins into my hand. "Medium sweet, please," she said, swinging her chair around and turning back to her easel. I slipped my hands into my pockets and walked slowly to my desk.

By that afternoon, news had spread around the office and I found coffee orders taped to my desk, and I was bringing in trays of coffee for Lanka and all the other first-row artists. The saddest thing of all was that I didn't really mind.

The next day I sat in my squeaky chair, pulled a blank sheet off the easel, and peered at the drawing that had been behind it. They were at it again: Grandma and Grandpa had chairs strapped to their backs, and Nika yanked savagely at the bird-cage. A few of the canary's feathers had fallen into a puddle of yellow at the bottom of the cage, and the bird wasn't singing.

I sat in my chair and began to think things over. Maybe I had bad pencils. Maybe I had a bad heart and God, who knew such things, was punishing me. I hung my head, felt my eyelids flutter. Perhaps I dozed then, because I saw lime trees that had flowered to lorgnettes, dangling long with the hours. Then the Apostles came trumpeting out, one by one. Behind them I saw the hangover dog wagging his tail in approval. He let out a tremendous bark, the loudest sound imaginable, and then I felt a hand jogging my shoulder.

I jumped from my chair, clutching my heart.

"Relax," Arnos said, his fist to his mouth in preparation for another sneeze. "It's just my allergies," he said at last, taking a handkerchief from his back pocket. "Well, let's see them."

"Who?" I blocked his view of the sketches with my body.

"The Headwater Homes." Arnos returned his hand to his pocket and walked his other fingers over the corners of my sketches. He was only two boards away from discovering my family on the move. I dug my thumbs into my temples and groaned.

"See, you're drinking too much coffee. Look what it's doing to you—you're jittery and distracted." Arnos shook his head as he studied my cookie sketch for an account we'd lost months ago. "Have you thought of applying for a transfer?"

"A transfer?"

"I think your work is completely underrated," Arnos said.

"Really?"

Arnos thumbed through some of my old sketches and knit his brows in concentration. "Maybe not," he said at last, and walked away.

By the time he made it back to his desk, Grandfather, Grandmother, Nika, the canary, and the shaggy dog had set up residence in a summerhouse I'd drawn.

"Look, this can't go on," I whispered to Grandfather. "You've got to stay where you're put."

"We feel stifled," said Grandmother.

"We are restless," said Grandfather.

"Give us something better," Nika added. "Or else."

I took the No. 18 tram home. As the carriages bumped over the joins, I thought of all those doomed sketches for silly products, my dark flat filled with similar items that I had never known I needed: breath mints, air fresheners, electric can openers, even a toaster. The clutter, the waste, was enough to throw me to my knees. That and the endless list of things I had to do (clean the toilet, launder my shirts), yesterday's list so similar to today's. The whole idea of another day depressed me utterly.

"Slay me now!" I cried, throwing my hands in the air as I'd observed Mama doing all her days in our cramped flat. "Oh, life!" I shouted again, wagging my aching head from side to side. I noticed the other passengers had drifted to seats closer to the door.

I let myself into the flat and headed for Mama's special-occasion liquor cabinet, from which I poured myself shot after shot of bad vodka while I watched the evening trains. I might have fallen asleep if it hadn't been for Manager Koza, rapping on the door with his thick knuckles.

"Oh, Jiri! Jiri!" Manager Koza pinched my check between his fingers. His face had crumpled into a mess of furrows. "Your check," he said, holding it away from his body. "It's no good."

In the morning I awoke to the sounds of the concrete cracking, as if the entire apartment building were shifting on its foundation. As I pulled on my trousers, I decided I needed to sit closer to those windows at work, I needed to be able to watch the pigeons flute the edges of the panes with their wings as they came in for their landings and again as they lifted when the saints rang out the hours. I decided that watching their gentle departures and arrivals turn with the change of light and shadow might calm me, might settle me somehow.

After I had delivered coffee to the entire first three rows, I sat in my squeaky chair and pressed my thumbs against my eyes. I contemplated my unruly and ever more vocal Headwater Home family.

Lanka approached, empty coffee cup and coins in hand. She wore a skirt just short enough so that if I crouched under my desk, I might actually see something. I bent over in my chair and pretended to tie my shoe. She had a great walk. And then there she was at my desk, tapping her blocky-heeled shoes with impatience. I straightened and hit my head against the desk.

"Idiot!" Nika called to me from the easel.

"Shut up," I said under my breath.

"What?" Lanka blinked.

"I was just talking to myself," I mumbled, rubbing my forehead.

"You really should learn how to like yourself more," Lanka said. I wondered if that was a clue, the green light that meant she wanted me to ask her out. But I could see it in Lanka's eyes: she didn't understand me, for the most part, and she didn't like what she did understand.

She walked back to her desk, and I heard Nika laugh from the easel. "Loser," I thought I heard her say.

New Guy swiveled around in his chair and glared at me.

Later that day I took out the Headwater Homes sketch and addressed the family directly. "All right. Tell me what you want, and I'll draw it," I said.

Grandfather Vaclav dropped his hammer, and I saw Grandmother Treba stretch her lips, the closest she'd ever come to smiling. Nika's eyebrows rose in genuine surprise.

"Really," I said, "I mean it." I stuffed my hands into my pockets, and Nika opened her mouth and chanted a litany of everything anyone could ever want, real or imagined, a list she must have been memorizing before she even existed on the page.

I rubbed my hands together and then started drawing everything they wanted. I started with a miniature Petrin Hill, with cobblestones in the pattern of a horseshoe. I used my best paints, even mixed up a special clay red for the rooftops, because I wanted to show how the sun could warm the tiles, how the light made everything gentler, and how the heat rising in a haze turned the air thick, and how at twilight all is forgiven and the city becomes more tolerant.

I drew pear trees and fruit rusting on the vine, and a wrought iron bench for lovers because yes, everyone ought to have romance, even if it is on a miniature scale. I put geese in a little pond, geraniums at Grandmother Treba's window, and outside, big bushes of tomato plants, spots of lavender, a lime tree, and tiny Nuremberg pigeons that would leave their tiny, fish-shaped droppings on the tiny stones. And in the summer cottage I gave Grandmother Treba a kitchen anyone would kill for—it even had a refrigerator with a freezer compartment that made ice in little cubes. In the lavs, I drew self-flushing commodes, just as they had asked.

For a while they seemed content. Grandmother Treba stuck tufts of periwinkle in each of her buttonholes, Grandfather Vaclav propped a ladder against the side of the cottage and inspected his new roof, and Nika sat on a lawn chair and jiggled ice cubes in a glass of Fanta and chain-smoked. They looked so happy, each of them in a private sphere, that I wished I could jump in there with them, forget the headaches that they had caused me, forget the Hair of the Dog campaign, Good Soldier Svejk, New Guy, Lanka, and all the rest of them. But in the end I doubted that whatever magic, whatever strange rules of cosmogony or whatever it was, that governed them actually governed me. I went home, my back aching but my heart a little lighter, convinced I had done at least one good thing.

I had learned in school that the laws of the universe are simple, much simpler than we are inclined to believe. I thought of the law of returns and figured that my one good deed, my one little kindness, might one day come back to me. And so when Lanka approached me first thing the next morning, I felt giddy. Maybe, finally, the universe was repaying me a cosmic debt.

"Got a light?" she asked, leaning toward me with her cigarette in her mouth. Like me, she needed to smoke more than worry about Arnos's allergies. If anyone had seen us just then, they might have thought we were about to kiss. I thought about touching a lock of hair that had tumbled from behind her ear, but as I straightened she stepped back, and I realized then that my thumb was on fire. From my desk I heard Nika snicker.

"You're an angel," she said, puffing on her cigarette.

"No, I'm not," I said, leaning over and sticking my thumb into a cup of cold coffee in my rubbish bin.

"Have it your way," she said with a shrug, and then she was gone again.

I knew that I should be upset about burning my thumb, especially since I had burned the very place where my thumb guides my pencils, the specific part of my thumb that was paying my rent, but I wasn't. It seemed logical, natural even, that I should burn myself while lighting a cigarette for the beautiful Lanka, and logical that she shouldn't even notice.

I sighed and turned back to the Headwater Homes sketches. I was just a day and a half away from the deadline. I pulled back the cover sheet and studied the grandparents and Nika in their dream cottage. The more I looked at them, the more I thought that even now, with all this stuff, there was a sound of despair in the tinkling of Nika's ice cubes, and Vaclav's climbing up and down his ladder seemed dogged. Nika wasn't heckling me anymore, and Grandmother Treba had developed a bad habit of kicking the refrigerator, leaving little black scuffmarks on the bottom. The dog I'd given them moved listlessly from room to room, trying to find the right place to lie down, and the canary wilted on her little perch. True, since I had drawn their dream cottage the day before, I had ignored them a bit, but they had no idea of the terrible pressure the Svejk campaign was giving me, especially after I had had such a hard time getting the Hair of

the Dog campaign right. But overall, I couldn't quite understand their tacit state of despair. I had drawn and painted everything they had asked for, everything they had said they wanted.

I worked until 3 A.M., past all the last calls of the pubs, re-
touching my despondent family and their gloomy house. But
the more I drew, the more faded-out everything became, and
soon it began to look as if a fine dust were covering the
sketches. The dog wouldn't even lift his head from the kitchen
floor, where he'd finally settled, let alone wag his tail. Grandpa
Vaclav came outside holding a cabbage in one hand and leaning on his cane with the other. I thought that even the small
cabbage looked sad. Finally, at 5 A.M., I lay my head on my desk
and slept a dreamless, heavy sleep.

When I awoke a few hours later, the first thing I noticed was
that my sketchpads, canvases, and tackle box of paints were
gone. I looked around and saw that all my things had been
moved to the back corner of the office, behind the rows. New
Guy had my easel, and when I approached him, I could see that
he was working on Svejk. The soldier was standing at attention, his gold buttons and epaulets glittering over a royal blue
uniform. Under New Guy's hand, Svejk had never looked so
regal, so imperial, so un-Svejk-like.

A few moments later Arnos brought me a cup of coffee.
"Cute," I said, nodding toward Svejk.

"Look, Jiri, I can tell you're upset. But think of it this
way—you're better off without Svejk. You've been looking a
little spent, so maybe you can just focus on those Headwater
Homes sketches." Arnos crossed his arms and nudged my
shoulder with his. It was an old gesture, and I knew it meant
that in spite of everything, we were still friends.

I tried to reconcile myself to my new situation. I wanted to
put my failures behind me, but at my new desk Grandfather

Vaclav kept coughing and looking at me, shifting his weight from one foot to the other, waiting for me to notice him. Out of the corner of my eye, I saw Grandmother Treba dumping rubbish out the front door and stamping her feet at the pigeons. Lanka was headed my way, this time with a sketch in her hand. She was smiling, and I felt my heart leap. Then Nika whistled.

"For the love of God, what is it now?" I hissed at Nika, and Lanka froze in midstride, then slowly backed toward her desk. New Guy turned to look at me, and Dubcek readjusted his headphones.

"The geese are biting us," Nika said, showing me a nasty bruise near her ankle.

Grandfather Vaclav spoke up. "Our chimney is blocked," he said. "Sadness is dripping down the flue like a pitch and we are weary."

I feel it too, I wanted to tell them, but what the hell was I supposed to do? I put my elbows right in their lavender garden, held my head in my hands, and wept. My shoulders shook and my nose ran and my eyes watered. Their words had triggered a recognition of something I'd noticed in myself. Despair, I wanted to name it, for I was a useless artist, unable to attract women. I had disappointed my mother in ways I was only just beginning to understand, and was altogether an insignificant human being. And these words, these admissions—I had been avoiding them for years.

"Sorry, sorry," I said to the family. My tears had turned their yard into a muddy wash, and I did my best with a handkerchief to blot the color back into place. I could feel New Guy eyeing me, but I kept dabbing at the canvas. Grandmother Treba shuffled her feet and tamped down the mud.

"If it's not too much to ask, would you mind cleaning up the rubbish that's stacked up over here?" Grandfather Vaclav emptied his pipe against the heel of his boot and walked to the back garden.

I wiped my eyes, dabbed my brush with white, and painted over the heap of chicken bones and rotted pears beside him. The rest of the afternoon I spent appeasing the grandparents. I deepened the shade inside the house and brightened the sunshine outside. I used my charcoals on their faces to highlight their laugh lines and overshadow any hint of residual longing or disillusionment. When I'd had enough, when my fingers ached, I left my desk for a smoke and a trip to the lav.

When I returned, they were gone. Just like that. The house looked dingy and the yard dim and mottled. Dirty dishes were stacked in the sink, and on the back steps was Vaclav's broken hammer. I sat in my chair, pinched the bridge of my nose, and sighed. Suddenly their fading little house on the fading canvas seemed unbearably empty. I painted tiny white asters for the beautiful Nika. Then I rested my elbows on my desk, put my head in my hands, and closed my eyes.

The clock sounded, lifting the pigeons from the window ledges like Roman candles bursting into flight. Suddenly Arnos was at my desk, synchronizing his watch and asking for my sketches. "OK, let's have them," he said, holding his watch to his ear. Behind his shoulders, I could see the Apostles making their rounds.

"Hair of the Dog Hangover Remedy," I said, handing him the sketch of the long-haired dachshund with the ears standing straight up. The dog wore rhinestone-studded sunglasses, each lens reflecting a stein of frothy beer.

"Too silly," Arnos said. "And what are these smears doing at the bottom?" He handed the dog back to me. "What else have you got?"

New Guy now handled Svejk, and I couldn't let Arnos see the Headwater Homes piece, which seemed to be vanishing before my eyes. "That's it," I said.

Arnos unrolled a cough sweet from its wrapping and ground it between his molars. Behind him I could see New Guy, whom I now hated very much, watching with what seemed to me an inappropriate amount of curiosity. I wished then that I was Marek and that I had had the incredible foresight to keep cheap secondhand chairs around for smashing on these kinds of occasions.

"The thing is," Arnos said with a crunch, "we're up against a bit of a deadline."

I could feel my stomach waltzing sideways, and I thought I was going to be sick. "I have to go home," I said, clutching my stomach.

Arnos followed me to the lift, even pushed the down button for me. "Here," he said, handing me a yellow termination slip. "I'm sorry, Jiri. Really I am." Then he reached for my hand to shake it.

Now I'm coloring filmstrips for a company that makes educational materials for kindergartners and prison inmates. Even better, I sit in the third row. I don't want to sound like I'm bragging, because it's not as glamorous as everyone thinks, but I'm happy, so I really can't complain. At the end of the workday, my fingers are crusted in primary colors. And though there's something gratifying about the heavy ink of the strip dyes, sometimes I miss the possibilities of oils, of mixing my own paints, of the quality of translucence and light in watercolor. I'm not bitter, though. Not at all. And for this, I congratulate myself.

At night I go home and listen to the trains laboring over the tracks and watch the squares of light moving across my ceiling. I think of my Headwater Home family, of Nika, who managed to lounge with a sultry grace I can't find in any women here in this city. I think of Grandfather Vaclav, of his wilted cabbages; of Grandmother Treba, the black kick marks on the refrigerator, her drooping geraniums. I try to recall them fully, their fading faces, but they are quietly disappearing from my mind, a little more each day.

In bed I lie on my back, my arms pressed to my sides, and I watch the moon's slow pass illuminating the pocked topography of my ceiling. I think about the fixed boxes of the filmstrips. There are no people moving around inside them, though at times, when I'm filling in the bubbles, I find myself talking to the figures in the frames. "Don't look at me like that," I'll grumble, or, "You think you're so smart?" But usually it's something much simpler, like "Help." I could wonder how many nights I'll pass this way, waiting for another day to fold up quietly. I listen to Manager Koza rattling at the door ("Jiri—your check!") and the trains hoot and trundle over the tracks, and I tell myself I'm not defeated, not lonely, not with all this noise and bustling. In the morning I wake with a start, the thought that something unexpected, something magical even, might still happen to a guy like me, pulling me toward the city throbbing below the hills.

A Blessing

THOUGH THEY ALREADY HAD a cockatiel named Fluria, Vera and Nikolai decided to adopt a dog. They were thirty years old and decided, too, that caring for a dog might teach them things about raising children that owning a cockatiel hadn't. After all, Fluria was so self-sufficient that she hardly seemed to need them.

After scrutinizing the classifieds, where the dogs listed were all purebred and thus too expensive, Nikolai agreed to go to the local humane society on his day off. Vera, who couldn't go with him because she was temping in a dentist's office, felt sure that Nikolai would find a good candidate. "Not a big dog," she said, helping Nikolai into his cracked leather coat. As the door fell back into its locks, her voice trailed: "And not a black one!" It was her way, he knew, of referring to their old life in Siberia, where big black dogs roamed the streets and were rumored to maul small children.

In Novosibirsk, the best kinds of dogs were statues that lovers visited on summer evenings. It was considered good luck to write one's name and all that one hoped for on a slip of paper and stuff it into the metal dog's mouth. Real dogs there were likely to bite. In their old apartment building, all the dogs had been big, with dark, oily coats and sharp, eager looks in their eyes. And every one of them had been mean. But in Novosibirsk, a hard city of concrete and wind, if you lived in a bad neighborhood, as Nikolai and Vera had, it was necessary to keep such animals as watchdogs. The only people who didn't were those who could afford to live outside the city. And when Vera and Nikolai had graduated, each with a Ph.D. in engineering and the firm knowledge that there was no work for them in Russia, they left the new tenants Malka, the ill-tempered dog that had come with their flat.

Inside the Mid-Willamette Valley Humane Society, civic-minded calls to neuter and spay plastered the walls, along with scores of advertisements for products Nikolai had never imagined a dog might need: special antiflake shampoos, heartworm pills, and toys so elaborate that Nikolai was sure they were initially designed for children. A woman led him along a concrete strip through the holding area, where the animals were kept in pens so small that the dogs didn't even have room to lift their legs and pee with dignity. He stood for a moment listening to the cries and yelps. Most of the dogs had pinkeye, and a few held their tails at half-mast, as if their tails or their spirits had been broken. Without a word, Nikolai turned on his heel and walked past the volunteer workers hosing down the cement, past the civic-minded posters, and out into the blinding bright daylight.

The early winter sky was padded with clouds so white that Nikolai turned his gaze to his shoes and his thoughts to the winter skies of his youth. In Novosibirsk, the clouds, thick and deliberate, would stack up so quickly and completely, it seemed they'd been railed in on the Trans-Siberian or Trans-Turk line. Over there, a long and lowering bank of clouds meant snow, days and days of it. And in Novosibirsk, people did not react to snow as they did here in this temperate valley of western Oregon, where the lightest dusting threatened to shut down the entire town.

Nikolai stuffed his hands into his pockets and crossed the parking lot. In Novosibirsk they did not have humane societies. Unwanted dogs were left to roam the streets, unless they became too aggressive or bothersome, and then they were shot. If you wanted a dog, all you had to do was set out a dish of scraps. Then you'd have more dogs than you would know what to do with.

Nikolai kept walking until he was just a few blocks from his apartment building. He sat on a bus-stop bench and studied a plastic banner strung between light poles advertising karate lessons at "the School of Hard Knocks." Why anyone would wish to pay seventy-five dollars a month to have his ass kicked three times a week was beyond his comprehension, though Vera had assured him it was a strange corollary of the American Dream.

Nikolai flicked the butt of his cigarette and watched it land on the street. Five cigarettes later, he was thinking of giving up, of telling Vera there were no good dogs at the pound, when he heard a whimpering. Nikolai observed crows wheeling in tight circles around a dumpster. He walked over, shooing away the crows. Behind the bin he found the source of the sad noise: a puppy so young its eyes still hadn't opened. In another day it would starve, if it weren't first pecked and eaten by the crows.

Nikolai unzipped his coat, scooped the dog from the ground, and cradled it against his chest. Its breath was warm on his neck, and though Nikolai was not a smiler by nature, he could feel his face rearranging itself into something like a smile. He was happy in this moment, happy to know that something as small as finding a dog that needed finding could affect him, even just a little bit. Nikolai rested his chin on the puppy's head, felt the tiny bones of its skull against his jaw.

"Shura," Nikolai whispered. It was the diminutive of Alexander, the name of a strong, admirable man Nikolai knew. "If you make it through the week, I'm going to call you Shura."

When he returned home, Vera met him at the door. With her peroxide blond hair and wide-set Tatar eyes, hers was a severe beauty that even now, four years after the civil ceremony, made his breath catch in his throat.

"Look," she said. Before he had a chance to show her the puppy still tucked in his jacket, Vera handed him a fat envelope full of rubles. The return postmark showed an address in Nefteyugansk, the oil-rich Russian Far East. Nikolai peered into the open envelope. "There must be a mistake," Vera said, taking the envelope from Nikolai and slapping it on the kitchen counter. "It's from my second cousin on my mother's side. Why she is sending money to us, I can't imagine, especially since we never liked each other."

Nikolai, still carrying the puppy in his coat, went to the freezer for their special-occasion vodka. As he withdrew the bottle, Vera frowned, and he wondered at her tendency to remain gloomy in the presence of such unexpected windfalls, a tendency he attributed to all Russian women. Shura wriggled beneath his coat, and Vera pointed her nose and sniffed in his direction.

"What's that?" she asked.

Nikolai pulled open his jacket and showed her the puppy.

Vera stepped forward and held her breath, her hands frozen in midair as if she were about to sneeze. "You got this at the pound?"

"No. I found him by the bus stop."

"But street dogs are wild, you know that. They maul children."

Nikolai laughed. "Not this dog," he said, rubbing Shura's

fur, which reminded him of new snow, stark white with the exception of a thin black stripe that started at the tip of his nose and ran the length of his back. "He looks like he could be a Siberian husky or maybe a Malamute. Look at that mask—like a raccoon's."

Vera frowned. "But he's missing a tail. What's a dog without a tail?" She demanded, poking the puppy at the stump where a tail should have been. "How will we know if he's happy or not if he has no tail to wag?"

Nikolai shrugged. In truth, he hadn't noticed the missing tail, and now it hardly seemed important. He stepped beside Vera and placed Shura in the crook of her arm. At the feel of something warm and living, Vera's back went stiff. "He's so little, it's scary."

Two days after Nikolai brought him home, Shura opened his eyes and they saw that these were his most unusual features. One was brown and one a blue so pale it appeared white. At first Nikolai thought the dog was blind in the blue eye, and he wondered if the eye was a sign of bad luck.

When Vera held up Shura's chin, she marveled at how clearly she could see herself in his mismatched eye. But as she studied that eye, she swore she caught glimpses of unsettling things—the wide expanse of tundra and fescue, water refracting jigsaw pictures of the sky, endless water wobbling with no place to go.

"Shah! It's your imagination," Nikolai said with a wave of his hand.

The next evening Shura hid under their bed and whimpered all through the night.

"He probably misses his mother," Nikolai said, kneeling and attempting to coax Shura out by pulling a red string over the floor.

"It's as if he knows something is about to happen," Vera said, her eyes narrowing. But Nikolai, still on his hands and knees, merely shook his head and thought she'd begun to lose what little wisdom she'd had.

In the morning they found Fluria dead at the bottom of her cage. Nikolai picked her up by her wing and carried her out to the trash bin behind their apartment while Vera, cold to the core, climbed back into bed, pulled the covers to her chin, and wondered aloud what else Shura's arrival would bring.

As far as dogs went, Shura did not seem much out of the ordinary. He needed to be taken out for a walk once in the morning and once at night. He had a favorite toy, a mechanical mouse that he batted around the floor or carried by the tail everywhere he went. And though his ordinary behavior seemed to make up for his strange looks, something else about him set Vera's teeth on edge. What that was, exactly, she couldn't determine. But because she wanted to show Nikolai and herself that she could be a good mother if she put her mind to it, she often talked to Shura, holding him in the crook of her arm. She ran through her huge repertoire of stories, all of which were meant to illustrate the difficulties of living—the risks of hoping for too much, of expecting the days to satisfy you fully. "Suffering is, after all, the highest form of mercy," she'd admonish, pressing him to her heart so that he could hear its even beating. Despite her attentions, however, Vera could tell that Shura preferred Nikolai, was in fact as loyal to him as a stone to a cherry. Perhaps this was because Nikolai let Shura sit beside him on the couch while he watched soccer matches. *"Milii,"* Vera would say to Nikolai, *Sweetie,* her way of letting him know she was ready for bed, and both Nikolai and the dog would jump from the couch. Some nights Nikolai even let Shura into their bedroom, and the dog slept in a tight ball at the end of their mattress. These were the nights Vera lay awake, thinking of a dog in Kamchatka who had been elected the new mayor by popular vote. Such craziness occurred regularly in Siberia, and Vera supposed that Nikolai was just the kind of man who would vote for a dog if he could. These were the nights when, listening to Nikolai's full-throated snores echoed by Shura's flutelike whistles, Vera began to like her husband a little less.

One day Vera and Nikolai received in the mail a free subscription to *National Geographic* and another envelope stuffed with rubles from Siberia. With this and other money from her relatives, Vera and Nikolai decided to buy a new TV with basic cable service, a luxury they had never even dreamed of having. As the cable man hooked up their service and switched on the TV, she discovered that they had access to all of the channels, including a station that aired a program called *The Miraculous Handkerchief,* a show she watched while the cable man gathered his tools. In less than two minutes three different women testified to the healing powers of a little square-shaped cloth. Applying it as a poultice had cured the first woman of monthly female pains, and it had whisked away the migraines of the second woman. In the case of the third, the handkerchief was responsible for removing liver spots on her skin. Two minutes of this was all Vera needed to determine that it was a show she could not abide. In Siberia nothing was as unlucky as a piece of good luck. A windfall was a sure invitation to disaster, and all her life Vera had witnessed the extreme caution people took to avoid abundance. Nothing aroused her suspicion quicker than the suggestion of a miracle or even simple good luck. No sooner had she let the cable man out the door, tromp and wrench, than Vera brought up the matter of their continuing good fortune to Nikolai.

"What could this mean?" she asked.

Nikolai rolled his eyes heavenward and shrugged. "Maybe it's a sign that God is smiling on us," he said, pulling on his boots.

"God doesn't smile," Vera persisted, withdrawing from the toe of her boot a ten-dollar bill. "It's bad magic, and this dog is to blame."

Nikolai observed the hardening knot of small muscles along Vera's jaw. "We should be on our hands and knees thanking our lucky stars for a dog like this. He doesn't bite, he doesn't bark, he doesn't beg, and he even kicks up the dirt to cover his messes so we don't have to pick them up. So what if he looks a little strange?"

"Nikolai, your *r*'s—you're rolling them again." Vera said, pulling on her other boot.

"And you are dragging your long Siberian shadow behind you." Nikolai threw up his hands. "He's a good dog. What are you so afraid of?" Nikolai knelt beside Shura and scratched the thick white fur on his chest.

Vera leveled her gaze on Shura, remembering wintertime tales from Siberia of hungry wolves in the woods and over-turned sleds. "Good dogs can easily turn bad," she said at last.

Vera awoke one night to the sound of scraping and scratch-ing. Mice, she thought, and when she switched on her bed-side lamp, the scratching ceased. She was tempted to shrug the noises off, but as she settled back beneath the covers, her eyes fluttered and she heard the soft dropping of rain and the beat-ing of wings. "Fluria?" Vera called, even though she knew these were not the sounds of a cockatiel. The scratching started up again, only this time it was much louder, and Vera bolted up-right.

"Kolya—wake up!" She jabbed at Nikolai with her elbow.

But he was lost in a thick, unshakeable sleep. From outside their window she heard a loud wailing that seemed to rise and fall with the beating of the wings. Vera crept to the window. On the street below she could see twenty, maybe thirty dogs, huddled together, dark as soot. They threw their heads back and continued to howl and bay, but at what she could not tell. The fog was as thick as fish soup, and she couldn't see the moon. She wondered if the neighbors in their building could also hear the noise, and she held her breath, listening for the sounds of human stirring. But all she heard was that scratching and the throaty calls of dogs.

Vera pulled on her slippers, went to the kitchen, and switched on the light. There was Shura, his front paws tapping the window, his nose pressed to the pane.

Vera snapped her fingers. "Shura. Come!"

At the sound of his name Shura turned, cocked his head, and regarded her for a moment. He flattened his ears and wagged his stump of a tail, but he didn't leave the window. It was the only time Shura had disobeyed her, and Vera felt certain it showed a fundamental wildness in him she would never be able to control. And for the first time since Shura had come to their apartment, she felt actual fear. Her whole body was seized with it as if she'd swallowed a fist.

When Vera awoke the next morning, Nikolai had already gone to work. Vera took Shura for his walk, and there were no traces to be found of the huge pack of dogs. She was tempted to forget the whole incident. Who would believe such a strange story anyway? But by the time Nikolai came home from work, Vera had changed her mind. She described the pack of dogs and the way Shura at the window watched them.

"Maybe they wanted him to come out and join them," Nikolai said evenly.

"No—that's not it. It was like he's their leader or something. You should have heard the noise they made." Vera held her hands together.

"What the hell do you want me to do about him?" He was rarely sharp with her, and she felt her face flushing.

She shrugged. "I don't like the idea of this dog anymore, that's all I'm saying."

Every night that week, the pack of dogs convened below the windows. Nikolai snored steadily in bed while Vera sat in her rocking chair and considered Shura, his ears up and his nose pressed to the window, or curled on the floor in a tight ball, his feet quivering with dreams. She wondered what images moved behind that placid blue eye, tugged at his twitching feet. Did he dream about other dogs? Did he want to be out there with them, roaming the streets and driving the neighborhood cats away? Did he notice stars in the sky, and if he did, could he detect in that ocean of cold geography and ancient logic a parallel map of hunts and chases? They were impossible questions, but she couldn't help wondering, and wondering too how it was that a pack of dogs could gather in the middle of night and carry on with their howling and baying without rousing one other single soul. Maybe she was hallucinating. Maybe there was nothing at all going on and her own mind was playing silly tricks on her, her female hormones flaring up in strange ways.

At first she attributed her loss of appetite to a common flu that for some reason wouldn't let go. But after several nights of intense headaches she knew it was something more serious. Going to a doctor was out of the question—she knew a doctor's only business was to deliver bad news. But she did consider taking Shura to the vet. For every pound Vera lost, it looked as if Shura lost two. He began to look so sickly that Vera gave him table scraps, even choice pieces of meat, but he continued to lose weight. She felt herself moved to something like pity for the dog. But then she'd look at him and instantly turn angry. All she required or expected of him was that he eat, shit, and be happy, and his refusal to do these things seemed to her further evidence of his wildness.

"Eat—eat if you know what's good for you," she'd say, prodding him with her foot. Through her thick stockings she'd feel the barrel of his bony ribcage. He'd gaze steadily past her, as if he were looking beyond the room. The blank sweep of his stare somehow transported her to the flat land where, whatever the season—an ice field in winter, a trembling *solonchak* of salty mud in summer—a person might walk and simply disappear, the land's uncertain skins having failed beneath her feet.

A few weeks passed and Vera regained her strength. She even felt well enough to redye her hair platinum, and she took pleasure in the fact that the biting smells of the chemicals didn't bring bile to her throat. But her relief was short-lived. The following weeks brought all manner of surprises. In the mornings, as she looked over their accounts, she discovered with alarm that their bills had mysteriously been paid, their debts forgiven. As if this weren't frightening enough, the doorbell would not stop ringing. First came a dozen roses meant for a woman at the end of the hall who had moved away but left no forwarding address. On another day, a man in a brown uniform delivered an enormous basket filled with pears and apples and chocolate from secret admirers, "Harry and David."

"Who's Harry? Who's David?" Vera asked Nikolai, showing him the baskets stuffed with Anjou and Bosc pears, which she knew at this time of year could sell for as much as three dollars apiece.

"Who cares?" Nikolai said, feeding a pear to Shura and wiping at the juice that dribbled from his muzzle.

But as the flowers and chocolates and fruit kept arriving, Vera felt her mood souring by degrees. Never mind that she had suddenly developed a fierce craving for these pears and candy. The sheer abundance, the inexplicable plenitude, was fraying her nerves completely. She could not help recalling an ancient Siberian saying: Whatever one is given is almost certainly taken away twofold.

Spring arrived, as did the slowly returning birds and the incrementally lengthening days. But Vera was too tired to notice. The dogs kept her up all night, and once again her stomach was failing her. She was three weeks pregnant—all three of her store-bought tests said so—and she was preparing to tell Nikolai, even had gone so far as to buy him more special-occasion vodka, when she had an epiphany. She was not the sort of person to have epiphanies, this much she knew about herself, so she took her small revelation seriously. It was early in the morning, so early that Nikolai was still burrowed deep in the blankets and muttering, determined to spoon up every last bit of his predawn dreaming. Vera hadn't slept a wink, and Shura had approached her, his ears up and eyes bright, and she knew that he wanted her to pet him. She reluctantly brought her hand down, ready to stroke his fur. As she brushed the longer hairs, she pulled back her hand and curled it into a fist. She couldn't touch him these days without looking into that blue eye and seeing brackish water and mire, dark ground yawning open, and the weight of her own body driving her down. She'd spent her whole life trying to get away from that landscape and here it was now, in an apartment eight thousand miles away, unfolding in the pale eye of her dog.

"This dog has to go," Vera said later that morning to Nikolai as he was leaving for the gym. The way she said it, her voice

measured but tight, made Nikolai suspect that there was something else she wasn't saying.

"I thought we agreed a dog would be good for us." He
pulled on his coat.

"He's not good for me."

Nikolai noted her stance: her back rigid, her elbows out,
her fists on her hips, her eyes hollow and hard. "We could give
him to someone else in the building," he said quietly.

"No. I don't ever want to see him again," Vera said.

Nikolai took in a sharp breath through his nose. "You could
take him to the humane society."

Vera shook her head, trying to imagine who in their right
mind would adopt such a dog.

"Do what you want, then," Nikolai said at last, gripping the
handles of his gym bag tightly, "but it's on your head." As he
left for his first session of those pricy karate classes, he was
struck by how strange it was that she could love him, her husband, but couldn't love something he loved. In their four years
of marriage he had never doubted her heart, her capacity for
finding room in it for the things that mattered, until now.

As dusk materialized, Vera weighed her decision. Shura sat at
her feet, his nose pointed to the window. She did not want to
be a hard woman doing selfish things. And she'd almost talked
herself into accepting Shura, as odd as he was, and just letting
things be, when the dog turned to her, wagging that stump
of a tail. *Don't look in his eye,* she told herself. *Blink.* But she
couldn't keep from staring at it, and suddenly she saw the face
of her grandmother there, her dark eyes wide with fear and her
hair coarse like wheat. The woman's features slowly rearranged
themselves to reflect the image of Vera, distorted as if from the
back of a spoon, her face bloated and her lips puffy.

"OK. That does it," Vera said, scooping up Shura and sling-
ing his front legs over her shoulder. She carried him down

the three flights of stairs and around the back of their apartment building. She didn't wring his neck as she wanted to,
or throw him from the freeway overpass, knowing that he'd
never survive the fall. Instead she carried him like a child in
her arms down their street. For over a mile she carried that dog,
until, out of breath and with her back aching, she half slung,
half threw him onto the sidewalk. She wiped her hands and
stamped her feet all the way back home. And she cried—a little
for Shura, but mostly for herself. She had failed, she knew,
and now she wondered how she would ever be able to love a
child the way she ought to.

When Nikolai returned home from the gym, he found Vera
sitting at the window. She was wearing her ratty blue bathrobe,
and he noticed for the first time how long her hair was getting,
how deep the hollows under her eyes.

"Are you feeling all right?" he asked, taking off his overcoat.

Vera looked at him. "I put Shura out today." She almost told
him she was pregnant, but she could see that already he was
wondering what sort of a person she was, what sort of a mother
she'd be now that she'd done this terrible thing.

Without a word, Nikolai turned, shrugged back into his
coat, and stepped into the hallway. He would go and enroll in
more karate classes. True, he might get his jaw broken, but at
least at the gym he knew what he was in for.

Vera did not miss Shura a bit. The pack of dogs went away, and
everything seemed almost normal again. Though she still slept
lightly through the night, she actually smiled with relief when
she heard the mice scratching in the walls. Here was one more
thing that had gone back to normal. She was just about to tell
Nikolai about her big news when small miracles started to oc-
cur once more. She found silver dollars in her shoes every
morning, and Nikolai began to smell the scent of roses in full
bloom even though it was only March. They won small and

large cash prizes from sweepstakes they did not recall entering, and they regularly received free samples and promotional gifts through the mail. They were instructed by the postmaster to keep them, in accordance with a finders-keepers law they'd never heard of.

Vera dreamed of a friend from Kursk swallowing a cat. Around midnight, while the woman slept, the cat stuck its paws into her open mouth and crawled down her throat. She awoke, unable to breathe, unable to scream, a terrible weight in her chest. But the cat continued the descent into her lungs, where it started breathing for her. Vera sat up in bed. She began to think she had felt Shura's warm breath on her face, his paw on her mouth. She pushed the covers back and swung her feet to the floor. She caught her balance against the bedframe as she carefully reached toward the mattress. There was a small depression in the blankets, as if Shura had been there, curled up and sleeping.

"What's the matter? What is it?" Nikolai cried when he woke and saw how pale her face was.

"Nothing. Just a very bad dream." Vera reached for her blue bathrobe and put it on.

Nikolai studied his wife. "Maybe we should move. Maybe we should just leave here, leave everything behind and go back to Siberia."

Vera touched her throat and sank to the bed. She still couldn't shake the feeling that her failure to love Shura signified a larger failing on her part. "I'm not a bad person." She turned to Nikolai. "Am I?"

He sat next to her and raised his arm as if to put it around her shoulders, but then let it fall to the bed. It's odd, he thought, when you can't think of one thing to say to your wife, not one, let alone the one thing that might help. He had loved Shura, had found in him a companion who loved him in return as only a dog can, simply and completely. He was sorry that Vera couldn't like Shura or at least tolerate him. And Nikolai was angry too, angry that Vera's limitations cost him, that she couldn't accept good things for what they were, and because of it others had to suffer. He grabbed his tobacco papers from the nightstand and moved his mouth, trying to find the right thing to say. "We could get another pet, a quieter pet, like a fish, maybe."

"No," Vera said, pulling her robe tighter around her. She was thinking of ice fields again, of feral dogs and long winters and endless snow. "No more pets." Suddenly she was very tired and sick of talking. She hoisted herself from the bed and padded toward the bathroom. "Besides," she called over her shoulder, "I've been meaning to tell you, I'm pregnant."

Nikolai held his cigarette between his forefinger and thumb and watched the paper burn to ash. He couldn't help feeling as if some strange joke had been played upon him, and then he felt guilty for thinking such a thing. He knew he should feel something, happiness or joy, but he felt sad, and then sad for feeling sad. He crushed the stub in the ashtray on his nightstand, determined to not be angry, not to hate his wife a little. After all, hadn't they wanted a baby all along? And this incredible gift they'd been given—wasn't this just one more evidence of heaven's generosity?

"Vera," Nikolai called, starting for the bathroom, where he could just see the edge of her blue robe.

Vera stood in front of the mirror, checking her stomach in profile. Already, she thought, she was losing her figure. She would bear the nausea and aches. Pregnancy was, after all, a suffering that a woman spends her whole life recovering from. And this thought brought comfort, that her pregnancy could be a severe form of mercy, and that this child might represent a second chance. In the mirror's return, she saw Nikolai advancing. She felt her stomach stir, the flutter of wings.

When the Dark Is
Light Enough

LUSYA VALENTINA ARTOV, age seventy-three, lay dying
on her kitchen floor, blinking in wonder at the gold flecks in
her ceiling, something she had never noticed until now. That
such small discoveries could still be possible seemed a funny,
unexpected gift. Grateful for this, Lusya tried to recall the ridiculous events that had led to her current position, her body
splayed on the floor, her heart folding up like a Chinese lan-
tern. She thought her situation had something to do with her
nephew and full-time border, Ivan. He'd been on the back
steps shouting at the top of his lungs, as he did so often these
days, and then the kitchen door had flown open and the doorknob had caught her on the hip. After that she slipped into
a solid, dreamless sleep. When she came to, she remembered
her bony aunt Triforov and how a broken hip so often spelled
doom. And yet Lusya could hear her canaries still singing.
Thank God for the tiny mercies—they were singing as if nothing had happened.

Lusya drew a sharp breath through her nose. Her heart stut-
tered and stopped. Then she felt a strange but painless split
somewhere behind her chest, and her spirit pulled away from
her body as if it were an old sheet of silver unpeeling from the

back of a mirror. Lusya bent over her still body and peered at her eyes reflecting the ceiling. She cocked her head, folded her arms across the small shelf of her stomach. She liked how her earthly body lay, arms outstretched, flung open as if she might fly off. It was not how she'd expected to die, but she was pleased, and her only regret was that Ivan was not with her in these last moments.

When the crime-scene processors set the large black trash bag on her worktable with a loud *thunk,* Karen rolled her chair over to it. Normally evidence came in paper bags, the kind mothers used for their children's lunch, or in grocery-size brown bags for bigger items like a soiled shirt or a stained pair of jeans. A trash bag this large usually meant trouble. Karen fingered the yellow laminate tag:

EVIDENCE A
Dog, species Siberian husky, stuffed

She untied the bag and peeled it back slowly to reveal the animal, a large dog that looked like a wolf.

"Who would stuff their dog?" Nick snorted and turned for the cooler. He worked at the table next to hers.

"Lots of people." Karen ran her gloved hand along the stiff fur of the ruff, over the bristly guard hairs along the dog's back. The glass eyes were a bright cerulean blue. Karen tapped an eye with her fingernail.

"It's evidence. Don't get too attached." Nick opened the metal door of the cooler. A cloud of cold wafted from within, and as he wheeled out a corpse, the cold made Nick's short, dark hair stand at attention, giving him the look of a frightened man.

Karen unsnapped the metal hasps of her toolbox and lifted the lid. In a single motion the three tiers of trays with all the carefully organized compartments yawned open. She reached for the fifty-power magnifying piece and began making a slow sweep over the dog's coat. Then she dipped a cotton swab in fluid indicator and rubbed at a soft red spot on the side of the dog's snout. When the end of the swab turned pink, signaling the presence of blood, Karen set up her trays for amino dye blots.

The trick with quirky evidence such as a portion of a jawbone, a child's bloodstained toy, or a stuffed dog was to act unsurprised, for this was the only way to keep the bile down and the nerves calm. It was something she'd learned to do while working at Dr. Van Meter's Canine Clinic.

Van Meter's clients were almost always dissatisfied housewives unable to control their dogs. What would Karen suggest? the women would ask. And with a quick turn of their heads they'd quietly refuse what she offered, the literature on rescue societies or dog obedience classes. Karen quickly learned that these clients were really asking her to agree with them, console them, then give action to what they dare not voice.

It never took long. The dogs, calmed by Karen's voice and her hand running over their coat from crown to tail, easily settled on the table. She always suspected they knew exactly what was happening to them, for dogs had a sense of their own time, she believed. And their breathing would slow, their bodies slump, the light behind their eyes dim.

In the long Siberian winters, the light left the days early and arrived late in the mornings. There in Yakutsk, where darkness bled the land for so many months of the year, Lusya learned as a little girl lying still in her bed to like darkness. It was in the inky shadows of twilight that she could imagine the full range of possibilities an object or a person suggested: a lampshade was the moon, a bar of soap a disk of silver, the family icons on the walls dim portals into heaven. Now, through the small glass window in the metal door of the cooler, Lusya could just make out a puddle of light and the faintest sound of voices. When a man opened the cooler door, a bolt of light made a sharp seam in the thick darkness. While the man jostled a metal gurney with a larger man's body on it, Lusya slipped past him.

On the long stainless steel table next to the bay of sinks sat Lev, her beloved Siberian husky. Lusya wrapped her arms around his thick neck and buried her nose in the bristly fur of his ruff. Lev had never been a smart dog, had managed to poison himself several times, but Lusya had loved him as if he were her child.

At the end of the table, a woman worked over a series of trays. Lusya narrowed her eyes, deciding to like the woman, *Karen,* her tag read, for she was like Lusya: all fingernails and toes, eyebrows and dental work. She was a collection of small parts and because of this was clearly mindful of the details, working slowly with hands that were quick and sure. Still, Lusya wanted to tell Karen to stop biting her lips, to remind her that such gestures advertised how completely unreconciled with her body she was. Lusya watched Karen pick up something that looked like a turkey baster, only smaller. With smooth squeezes of the bulb, Karen filled the lanes of a tray with blue gel. Not a bad-looking woman, but there was something sad about the way she bent over the lanes, as if nothing else in the world mattered.

What bothered Nick most about Karen was her voice, which struck him as plaintive but also too eager. Then there was the matter of her hair, which was an odd shade of yellow, not blond, not platinum, but yellow like corn. She wore it in a braid that was as thick as a limb and hung over her shoulder. It was her habit to move the thing from one shoulder to the other at the end of a sentence or just before starting a new task. Nick thought it was a sort of subconscious punctuation she supplied to her every thought or action, and if Nick was in the middle of a sentence and Karen reached for her braid, he knew the conversation was over.

For these reasons and a few more he couldn't name, Nick had cultivated a low-grade dislike for her that hadn't faded in the twelve months they had worked together. You'd think she was the prosecutor, Nick mused as he target-pissed at the drain holes in the urinal of the men's basement toilet. The way she kept on obsessively about her latest case, this Russian woman, you'd think Karen was the one who had been battered and left dead in her own kitchen. Nick zipped his fly and headed down the long hallway, past the laundry room that smelled of soap and lemons, past the hematology and toxicology labs, which, curiously, had no scent at all.

He elbowed through the swinging door and headed for the cooler. He had a midlifer inside, a supposed suicide with a suspiciously angled gunshot wound to the head. The man had been found with his glasses on, a rarity at the scene of a self-inflicted shooting.

"I'll bet you didn't know *lividity* is one of the few forensic words with roots that can be traced through several languages." Karen followed Nick to the cooler. Postmortem lividity was Karen's passion, and no matter what Nick said to steer the conversation away from it, nothing deterred her from her detailed descriptions of core body temperatures, speed of progression, how rigor mortis came and went. "French *livere,* Latin *lividus.* In Latin it means black and blue, but in Old Slavonic *sliva* literally means plum." Karen pulled the gurney with the dead Russian woman into the lab. "See!" She brightened as she pointed with a latex finger to the bruising at the dead woman's neck.

"Neat." Nick rolled his eyes and turned back to the dead man.

They used to be chummy, used to go for drinks after work. It was the only way to ease the horror of unwrapping FedEx boxes filled with hands or fractured skulls found in the woods or roadside ditches. Not a week went by, it seemed, that a woman's body didn't turn up raped, strangled, or sometimes worse, and it was Nick's job to probe for DNA evidence anywhere he could find it: in the mouth, in the stomach, under the fingernails, in the vagina. He couldn't help feeling complicit in the crime and somehow part of it, the worst kind of voyeur, only adding to the injuries as he documented them for the prosecutor's office.

The trick, he'd learned, was to remind himself that he was a professional, and an important one at that. After all, wasn't he the one most frequently requested at crime scenes and for autopsies? And didn't he know the unlikelihood of finding an easy clue, how evidence could be like a ghost, there one second, then gone, carried off by the wind or crushed by the careless tread of a detective's shoe? He knew the importance of patience, of allowing the possibilities to pull on him. He could determine in the drip and spray patterns of blood the direction of the blow, the type of weapon used, and with what force, what velocity. He could read how rigor mortis played on the body, starting with the eyelids and moving to the jaw. He had smelled the bitter almond scent of cyanide, had floated the lungs of water victims in a tank to see whether death had occurred before or after the body entered the water. He had even uncovered the corpse of an infant buried in a shallow grave of kitty litter.

Seeing these things, he couldn't escape realizing how very fragile the human body was. He had tried explaining to Shari, his ex-wife, what it felt like to perform these final ministrations, advocating for the dead while dismantling them bit by bit. He wanted to explain how the splay of the ribs lifted off like a shield or, with the shearing of the saw, snapped apart like a corset. He wanted to tell her that despite the actual fact of death, there was a beauty to all this activity, a dark but just grace to his busy examinations here in the bowels of the hospital. But he could never tell Shari any of this, for she could not bear his stories, no matter how poetically or plaintively he told them. There was something intrinsically antisocial about his kind of work, Shari claimed, walking away from him with her palms pressed over her ears. Nick suspected that she was afraid some startling detail might force her to consider the natural limits of life, and that her own days had a number was unthinkable.

For all these reasons and because he hated going home to his empty apartment and sitting through the long hours of the evenings and nights alone, Nick sometimes asked Karen out for a beer. He could tell by her hunched shoulders, her too-quick laughter, that Karen was like him — as lonely as God the day before he created man. He imagined that she went home at night to chain-smoke and watch bad cop shows, eat takeout, and find ways to convince herself that she was really living. It was Nick's conviction that if they got drunk enough, he might find at least one likable thing about her. But invariably he would bring up Shari, how she drank too much and tended to ignore their two children, preferring instead to troll the Internet and chat with other disgruntled and bored housewives.

"Some people shouldn't have kids," Nick remembered saying to Karen the last time they went out. He stirred his drink with his finger, brought his eyes to bear on Karen's. He couldn't help it and he knew it wasn't fair, but in the dim light of the bar she began to resemble Shari.

· · ·

EVIDENCE B
Woman's fringed scarf, stained

Delighted to see the care with which Karen combed over her prayer scarf, Lusya stood beside her and fingered the fringe. It had always been Lusya's favorite, this periwinkle-colored scarf with the careful embroidering in Old Slavonic: "And he shall give his angels charge over thee." As Karen scoured for fiber evidence and circled the stains on the scarf, Lusya pulled up a stool. She watched Karen treat each stain with a series of amino die blots. With a single drop of the dark substance, a faint blotch turned brilliant purple, revealing grooves and whorls, and Lusya realized with a start that Karen had just raised a print from the protein. For the rest of the afternoon Lusya tiptoed around the lab, marveling at the soft alchemy of gentian violet, ionized copper, and gold dust and the illuminating powers of ordinary Superglue when heated in an airtight chamber. She shook her head in wonder, sure that she had stumbled upon the stuff of stars spread out in ordinary dishes and vials on these tables.

Lusya watched Nick roll a middle-aged man toward the cooler. When the gurney slid clean through her body, Lusya wobbled on her feet and steadied herself with a hand on Karen's elbow. Strange, she thought, as she headed for the cooler, how in this overbright light of the medical examiner's lab she was indiscernible to Karen, whose eyes were so keen. Strange, too, how the man in the cooler, who greeted her with a quick nod—O'Malley, his toe tag read—and who, she noted, had a nostril-sized hole behind his ear, could see her clearly in spite of his shattered glasses.

The scorchmarks behind his ear intrigued Lusya, and she couldn't keep from staring at them. "What happened to you?" she asked.

O'Malley shrugged. "I don't know, but God, I could use a cup of coffee."

Lusya folded her hands in her lap, crossed her feet at the ankles, and tried again to remember her own final moments. With her eyes closed, she saw a flutter of white and brown hands the size of wrens at her forehead, heard the murmur of soothing words.

"It hurts," Lusya remembered saying, her voice distant like a mumble from behind a heavy curtain. "What happened?"

"Lots of things," answered a woman wearing a plastic visor. Then she leaned toward Lusya and whispered, "It's not fair." They must have been in an ambulance, Lusya deduced, because there was a strange wailing in her ear and somewhere farther off the pealing of church bells as well as the rumble of a train in the distance. Lusya looked for the color of the woman's eyes. But in the reflection of the plastic visor, Lusya saw an image of herself, a face neither familiar nor foreign, here nor there.

"Vasquez," Nick called out. It was a game with him, the closest he'd ever get to banter—he'd say a case name and drill Karen on the details to see if she knew them as well as he did.

"DMSO$_4$," Karen said, opening the cooler and rolling out the dead woman's body. Karen remembered the bizarre headlines on the Vasquez case: she was an asthmatic who went into shock when the paramedics administered oxygen. Her body then mysteriously began emitting a nerve gas, paralyzing the EMT in the ambulance. A few minutes after she was wheeled into the hospital, an entire ER crew fainted, and within an hour the whole first floor of the hospital had to be quarantined.

"They shouldn't have given her oxygen." Karen made a long incision at the base of Lusya's skull. Then she inched the scalp from the cranium, pulling it to the forehead and peeling the face down over itself. On the table beside Lusya, Nick subjected the dead man to the same procedure, though he had to stop to wipe the inside of the man's face with a towel to get a better grip.

"She shouldn't have lathered herself with Icy-Hot before she took her inhalant." Nick wiped his own forehead with another towel.

"How could she know it would react with the oxygen in her body?" Karen reached for the electric saw.

"The inhalant had nothing to do with it. She'd just finished chemotherapy. It was the residual chemo combined with Icy-Hot that triggered the mess."

"Sure." Karen nodded and leaned her weight into the handle of the saw, dovetailing the cuts so the pieces of the skull didn't move around while she was sawing. Then there was a wet crack and the skull sprang open.

From Nick's table came another loud crack, and with a pair of tweezers he extracted a spent shell from the man's skull, held it up to the light as if it were a precious gem, then bagged and labeled it. Karen bent over the open vault of the dead woman's cranium and touched the soft ridges of her brain. Which ridges carried her last dream? Where was the snapshot of that final moment, and when it happened, did she even see it coming? Karen wondered as she carefully fit the pieces of the skull into place and pulled the woman's skin like a mask back over it.

Nick craned his neck toward the dead woman. "Geez. What happened to her?"

Karen set the saw on the tray with a loud clatter. "Lots of things. Multiple blunt-force trauma to the head and face." She pulled back an upper lip to reveal a row of broken teeth. "Then we've got those ligature marks around the neck, fibers in the mouth and teeth, and hemorrhaging inside the neck and the eyes."

"Strangulation?"

"Yeah, but get this—yesterday I ran some blood and tissue

samples with the toxicologists, and there's evidence of heavy metal poisoning in the blood, on the hair follicles, and in the fingernail clippings."

Nick pulled the skin of the man's face back over the skull. "That's what I call overkill."

"That's what I call sick." Karen peeled off her gloves with a loud snap. An angry murder, that's what it was. Pure rage. A man, Karen decided. Only men batter the head and face so completely. It might not be fair to think such things, but Lord knew it was always the case.

"It's not fair," Karen whispered into the dead woman's ear. Then she took a few steps back and breathed through her mouth. The smell of burning bone was getting to her, and without a word she pushed through the metal doors to the quiet of the hallway.

Karen took another big breath through her nose and held it as she climbed the stairs. These were the moments, the blank spaces in the day, when she could feel her head quieting down and she could forget the bodies waiting for her below, the terrible answers she'd find lodged in the vault of a cranium. She opened the door to the roof and exhaled. Gone were the smells of the bodies that had failed, gone the stinging odors of chemicals that caused sudden headaches. Today the air smelled like a storm and the wind tore at her lab coat. Karen walked toward the hip-high concrete barrier that edged the rooftop. Up here she could see the graveled roofs of apartment buildings, retirement and funeral homes below, the pebbled tops of the buildings all a piercing white that forced her gaze to a squint. Then there were the rows of greenhouses blooming on top of the more important buildings. She would give anything to be among the topiaries, where someone had coaxed a privet hedge into the shape of a seahorse.

Karen stood, her hips against the barrier, and thought of the old lady on her table downstairs. There was too much sadness in this kind of work, a kind of unwieldy melancholy that sprang from examining so many lives through the sum of their parts and seeing the same human plots played out again and again. It was sad, too, that in her twelve months as a forensic pathologist, she had reached the same conclusion again and again: that death was the culmination of a lifelong cry for help.

Suddenly Karen felt envious, jealous in her very bones of the dead woman downstairs. She had pulled free from this life, had left this foolish, sad world behind.

Boredom made Lusya curious, morose, meddlesome. She asked O'Malley, "Will Ivan remember to oil the Christmas carp this year? Will he remember to ask Marya, not Lyuba, to lay out my body properly? And will Marya remember to bury me with a chunk of ice cradled in each palm for good luck?" But O'Malley didn't answer, and Lusya thought it must be on account of his liver, which had been sent to the toxicologist's lab.

The door swung open and light filled the cooler. Lusya lay back on the gurney, snug for a moment inside her own body, enjoying the short ride from the cooler to Karen's worktable. In another life she might have seen things differently, might have contented herself to buckle down and wait for the spirit to settle one knuckle at a time as it quietly rearranged itself. But not now. Now Lusya swung her legs over the gurney and helped Karen slide her body onto the stainless steel table.

It might have been an unhealthy curiosity, but Lusya really wanted to know exactly what had happened to her. She padded around the lab in her bare feet, occasionally looking over Karen's shoulder to read her careful notes: ocular petechia, a crushed hyoid bone, a positive result on a blood sample tested for heavy metal poisoning. What do these observations and findings all mean? she wanted to ask Karen. Yes, it was all there in black and white, in English, and yes, she was an excellent reader, but still, she had no idea what those words were saying.

When Karen reached for the saw, Lusya stepped back and covered her eyes with the prayer scarf, turning her attention to the careful stitching, the fringe. That this prayer scarf, such a flimsy thing, should outlast her brought her to laughter, then to tears. Lusya headed back to the cooler, where O'Malley was now grinding his teeth in his sleep. Later, when Nick shut the door, the light bulb switched off. A relief, really, an end to seeing, a combining of darkness with the designation of night.

On heavy, wet May evenings like these, evenings full with the possibility of a warm summer, Nick liked to sit on the edge of the loading bay behind the hospital and listen to the crickets. He would count the pairs of tennis shoes strung over the telephone wires. He liked watching the wind catch them, the way the shoes kicked a little in the breeze as if real feet might still be inside them. He liked the sound of the crows calling across the city blocks. Then there was the steady drop of sunset to night, the light shifting and revealing the blue hills just beyond the city and the ashen purple troughs between them, deep and inviolate.

This evening he could see across the buckled pavement of the parking lot to a small yard where a dog sat under a tree. Nick watched the dog, a big one, big like a great Dane. And old, too — Nick could tell by the way it moved its head slowly, watching the traffic go by. Nick watched the dog groom its oversized paws, licking the pads and nibbling on the tufts of gray hair around them. Watching the dog gave Nick some tiny pleasure. Only fifty yards from where bodies were loaded and unloaded, wheeled into the long sleek hearses of morticians, something lived.

Nick thumped on his chest, felt his own heart pumping. He thought of Shari, how with the lights out he used to love feeling the curves and smooth skin of her torso, knowing which rib her heart rested behind, which her liver. He loved the smell of her skin. He liked pressing his finger to the side of her neck to feel the throb of her pulse.

And then she was gone. Just like that. Leaving, she had told him, because their lives together had edged toward boring and she was frightened that at thirty-seven, saddled with two kids, she had become boring too.

In the cooler, where the darkness was just light enough to see shapes, Lusya prayed aloud for her nephew, Ivan. Would he be all right without her? Would he feed the canaries and sing to them the way they liked? Would he continue to eat those nasty TV dinners? She prayed to Saints Cyril and Methodius, her favorite saints. And both of them so smart! How they had managed to devise a written alphabet for people as unruly as the Slavs completely impressed her, and when she polished and cleaned the tiny Orthodox church, the icons of Saints Cyril and Methodius were the ones she kissed, sometimes twice. But when she lit candles, it was Ivan she thought of, Ivan she prayed for. If anyone needed it, he did: a boy still, at thirty, and mean, ordering her about her own home, commandeering her checkbook and even endorsing her checks for her. Still, she was convinced that if she said Ivan's name enough times, he would sense he was being prayed for, and her prayers would act like a magnetic force pulling him through time and space, bringing him to his knees, forcing a goodness in him and upon him.

"People just aren't interested in goodness anymore," Lusya whispered to O'Malley. No matter how many icons she'd made Ivan kiss, he couldn't seem to change his ways, and Lusya crossed herself fervently, begging that God's grace would overtake her poor foolish nephew in spite of himself.

O'Malley rolled toward her. "I'm really tired," he said at last. "Give it a rest, huh?"

"Sure." Lusya closed her eyes. Again she tried to recall the exact moment of her death, but she drew a complete and total blank. This struck her as funny for some reason. She had always imagined that in the final moment time would slow, then run backward, whirling her through her life, one memory at a time. She was disappointed that she had not had that stereoscopic moment, nor had she had visions or heard sweet sounds, though now that she was really paying attention, she thought she remembered a train rattling over the tracks and the mournful cry of a whistle.

"Are you moving this scarf around?" Karen folded a long sheet of butcher paper around the blue scarf and set the bundle in the evidence locker.

Nick shook his head and slipped his headset over his ears. "No."

Karen pulled out a small paper bag and turned her key in the lock. "I keep finding the scarf in the cooler."

Nick shrugged and fiddled with the volume control.

Karen placed the paper bag on her table, switched on her overhead lamp, and read the evidence label.

EVIDENCE C
One sock, multicolored

She held the sock to the light. A man's sock, she guessed from the size of it. Though she held it away from her nose, she could smell that it had been soured by chemicals. Starter fluid, maybe, but it would take hours, days even, at the tandem mass-spectrometer to determine which ones. Karen opened her toolbox and reached for her array of magnifying pieces.

• • •

When Lusya saw Karen handling the sock, she nearly fell off her gurney. She'd knitted that sock years ago for Ivan.

"No, no!" Lusya waved her hands in front of Karen's face, hoping that somehow she could stop her from seeing what she'd inevitably see. "No! You're making a terrible mistake!" But Karen continued to move the monocle in a slow sweeping pattern, her nose just inches from the sock. Lusya hung her head and made her way back to the cooler. Clearly she had more praying to do. And then she tipped her head to one side. As plain as day, she heard Ivan's voice, gravelly from too many cigarettes. Then he appeared, following a detective to the cooler, where her body lay beneath the green sheet.

"Is this your aunt?" The detective rolled the sheet down to Lusya's shoulders.

"Yes." Ivan's hand trembled at his nose and mouth. "When can I have the body? I'd like to have her cremated as soon as possible. It's what she wanted."

Karen's lips were pinched, and Lusya wanted to tell her to stop wagging her head balefully like that.

"We'll need to finish up some tests and paperwork first." Karen flipped on her overhead lamp.

"Tests?" Ivan asked. Lusya had never heard his voice sound so small.

"Yeah. Standard procedure for homicides."

"Oh," he said, his hand fidgeting with his belt.

Lusya pointed her nose toward Ivan and sniffed. She could smell blood and feathers on his hands, and soap too, but no matter how many times he might have washed, she knew what she smelled. How could her nephew, whom she loved, kill her birds? Yes, she knew times were bad for him. He had counted on her monthly social security check, had counted on her to cook and clean for him. But times weren't that bad, not bad enough to kill her poor pets. "Murderer!" Lusya cried, suddenly angrier about what he'd done to her birds than about what he'd done to her. She kicked Ivan's shin as hard as she could. But the detective just led him out into the hallway, where he bent and scratched his knee.

Lusya moved back to the gurney and slipped inside her body. With the sheet pulled over her head, her thoughts crumpled and new thoughts formed. In death as in life, she discovered with surprise, there was waffling. There was self-delusion. Lusya looked at O'Malley, who was now in possession of his much-maligned liver and blissfully snoring on the metal table opposite her.

"We're dead," she said to the sleeping O'Malley. "We're dead and there's nothing we can do about it."

O'Malley kicked at his sheet, rubbed his eyes. "I'm not so sure," he said, twisting on his gurney and grimacing. "Just look at those two." He nodded toward the door. "We're no different from them."

Lusya got up, pressed her nose to the glass, and studied Nick and Karen, each hovering over a microscope. She could understand O'Malley's confusion, especially watching these two fluttering around in their lab coats, rarely speaking to each other, slipping out for long breaks.

Lusya climbed back onto her gurney and pulled the prayer scarf over her eyes. It was wrong to ignore the truth. She wished she had a hand mirror and could crank O'Malley's neck hard to the left so that he could view the hole in the side of his head, could see the deep and fatal path that the bullet had taken. She considered telling him about the City of the Dead. It was an old story, but sound, and just the kind of thing you'd tell an exceptionally stubborn corpse. An old woman received a letter in the mail informing her that she'd won an expensive trip to a beautiful town in the south. The next day she put on her best clothes, and with that letter in hand she climbed aboard the train and traveled many hours. When she arrived in the city, a place called Cat's Mud, she could see straight off that something was horribly wrong. Everyone in the city was dead. It was clear to the woman how each of the people had died, for here was a man with a hole in his chest, there another, green and bloated, who'd obviously drowned. But they were carrying on with their business, smoking cheap cigarettes and sitting on park benches or standing in long lines—all this while wearing their funeral clothes and clutching their death certificates in their hands. When the woman tried to enlighten these people, they merely pointed at that letter of invitation in her hand and laughed, because she was dead too.

But Lusya feared that such a story would be wasted on O'Malley. Instead, she rapped a bony knuckle against the metal door. "We're really dead. Think about it." Lusya passed a hand through her body.

He shook his head in one savage motion from side to side. "No!" he screamed, and clutched his chest, frantically trying to push together the seams of his Y-incision.

Nick leaned back in his chair and studied the ceiling tile. He was tired down to every last fiber, and knowing that one floor above him in the ER people were suffering palpable traumas made him even sadder. He surveyed the racks of test tubes with variously colored rubber stoppers spread out before him. Next door was the Hitachi 912, a bulky machine with the look of a photocopier. He could hear it whirring away, parsing the tiniest traces of chemicals from serum and plasma. Now that O'Malley's kidney and liver and blood had been analyzed, Nick was lost in a flood of paperwork. A seemingly endless ream spewed from his printer to his desktop to the floor.

Karen stood at the sinks, scrubbing her hands. Beside her the pages of the toxicologist's report spooled around her feet. She squinted at the report header.

"Oh. Gun-shot guy."

"Yeah. Turns out he had enough tranquilizers in his stomach to knock out an elephant."

"So now what?"

Nick sighed. The sound awoke a strange feeling in Karen. Tenderness, it might have been. Standing behind him, seeing the muscles along his neck bunch up, made Karen suddenly want to touch him. Not in a sexual way, but sympathetically, a touch that might invite more touching should the occasion arise later.

"More paperwork." Nick laced his fingers behind his head and leaned back in his chair. "It's the chief medical examiner's problem now. The wife is bugging him to release the body. She wants to hold a big wake in their home, if you can believe it."

"I didn't know people still did that." Karen bent near the printer and retrieved the folds of paper flapping this way and that, like an accordion. She stacked the report on the edge of Nick's desk. She decided to help Nick in any way he'd let her, for there were days—and clearly this was one of them—when they both needed some sign, some evidence that there was such a thing as simple human kindness.

The next day the sheet covering her was as heavy as brick. Lusya could barely open her eyes or turn her head. She was grateful when Karen rolled her out and turned down the sheet in a single deft motion. It occurred to Lusya that she could easily leave if she just pushed through the swinging door and into the brightness of the corridor. But she was tired, too tired to move, and the fact that she couldn't fully escape her body's limitations astonished her anew. Lusya closed her eyes. She tried to remember her soul first rising, but she could think only of its weight, volume, density. And then what was the soul but another type of a body, and therefore proof that the body is, was.

· · ·

Up on the roof, Karen considered Nick's habit of running his hands through his hair, as if making sure it was all still there. It was a sweet gesture she'd come to count on, one of those little things he did that made her think she could almost imagine going out with him. But he was too good-looking, too capable for her, she decided at last. An ugly man, that's who she needed. Ugly men forgave more. Or maybe a fat man. Or a man so ruined by some horrible past that he was completely comfortable with love, needed it and would take it anywhere he could. Karen picked up a pebble and threw it as hard as she could toward the arched top of a greenhouse across the street. Below her she heard a car accelerate, then the driver grinding on the gearshift. Each night she went to her apartment, walked into the kitchenette, and stood there in her flannel pj's, looking out the window at the lights of the city. She recalled the many nights she had overheard the couple next door arguing or making love. She'd rattle the kettle on the range and turn on the TV just to make some noise of her own. Later she'd lie in bed, replaying the grim histories of the many bodies waiting for her in the morgue: the hysterectomies, the removed appendices, C-sections and signs of open-heart surgeries. She'd wait for sleep to come. Sometimes she'd press her finger against her carotid, just to make sure there was still a pulse.

She whipped her braid from one shoulder to the other. Behind her she heard the ominous shearing of a helicopter nosing toward the helipad. Starlings and rooks shot past her. She pressed her hips against the barrier, unaware that three stories below Nick stood in a similar position at the edge of the loading dock, watching the crows drift toward the telephone wire, clapping their wings once, twice, then settling. He saw an orderly wheeling out a body in a zippered body bag. And below he saw two hearses circling for the same spot. Sharks, Nick decided, the cars were sharks—each of them long and muscled, with fins over the taillights and slits that looked just like gills near the front wheel wells.

One of the hearses backed up to the edge of the dock and the driver stepped out. The man wore a three-piece suit and stood jangling his keys. Another man, young and equally impatient, got out of the passenger side and hurriedly opened the back door. Then he climbed the metal steps to the dock, brushed Nick's arm as he passed by on his way for the door. Nick unhooked his ID tag, stuffed it in the front pocket of his lab coat, and turned to the driver.

"You guys don't waste any time. The corpse is hardly even cold yet." They were here, he knew, for O'Malley, who he also knew was ready to go. But seeing the driver's impatience drew a rancor from Nick that he didn't know he had. Suddenly more than anything Nick wanted to hit the driver, knock him down with a solid punch and see him crumple to the pavement, see some sign of distress on his otherwise perfectly arranged face.

The driver looked at Nick, then checked his watch. "What's with you?"

"You guys make me sick, that's all." Nick took his hands out of his pockets.

The other man appeared with O'Malley on a gurney. At the lip of the dock he stood for a moment looking at the bag, unsure where to grip. Then he bent at the knees, hugged the bag to his chest, walked clumsily forward, and tried to shove it into the open hearse.

"Jesus H. Christ! If he hasn't been through enough already!" Nick went to him and grabbed at the bag. The man whirled on his heels, his elbow cocked. Nick felt the impact of the man's elbow on his nose, heard the loud crunch, and folded. He heard the scraping of the body bag sliding into the back end of the hearse, the car doors slamming, and the hearse pulling away.

Nick lay flat on his back and looked up at the hazy twilight sky. Three stories above him he saw a pale smudge, and when he looked closer, he saw it was the unnatural blond color of Karen's braid.

"Hey," Nick's voice floated up.

Startled, Karen jumped back from the ledge. Then she stepped forward again and leaned over the barrier. "Hey."

Nick fingered the bony ridge of his swelling nose. "How about a beer later?" he called up.

O'Malley was gone now, collected by a sharply dressed young man. Family, Lusya supposed, and she tried not to let it bother her that when Ivan had visited, he hadn't even worn a clean shirt. Lusya listened to the sound of a train, its wheels rattling over the joins. Now more than ever she wanted to pull free of the locker and follow the sound. But she couldn't even lift her head. She closed her eyes. Unruly memories blossomed forth, those stinging reminders of all that she needed to forget: Ivan, Lev, the many icons in need of kissing.

She became grateful for every breath, every last thought, every sensation. Yes, grateful for every moment, and just as grateful that it all finally came to an end. It was not like the graceful deaths in movies, or the kind people wrote poems about, but she wasn't bothered. No. It was just right, just the way she suddenly remembered: hazy and beautiful in its refusal to clarify into anything beyond the wet trilliums drowning on the hillside behind her house. At last, a bona fide vision. Lusya smiled. Then darkness, and Lusya had never been so glad to be left to it.

At a stoplight Nick rolled a small piece of tissue between his forefinger and thumb, then pushed it into his nostril.

"What happened to you?" Karen pulled open her purse and searched for another tissue.

Nick smiled and pushed at a loose tooth with his tongue. "Nothing."

They drove in silence for several blocks. Beside the concrete median to their left a small black dog lay on its side, crumpled and stiff. Karen thought of the many dogs she'd watched die at Van Meter's. She supposed those were gentle deaths, generous deaths. But not the way a dog would want to go. Not quietly like that, but caught lock-kneed in a full run, knocked clean from this life, from breath.

Nick turned the wheel, and the tires crunched over the gravel of the parking lot in front of the bar. "What a sorry, awful world this is," Nick said at last, pressing his palms to the steering wheel. Beyond the windshield the orange and green neon sign of the bar winked on and off.

Karen supposed Nick was thinking of his ex, or maybe of the dead man, O'Malley. She closed her eyes and suddenly thought of Lusya Valentina Artov, whose rigor mortis had caught her smiling in spite of a mouth full of broken teeth. Karen recalled how when the woman had been wheeled into the lab, her arms had been flung open. They'd looked like wings.

She squinted at the light coming from the neon sign, then looked at Nick. "No, it's not."

Signs and Markings

Men dream of flying because they thirst
for a state of mind where they need not
worry about the placement of their feet.

—RICHARD GROSSMAN,
The Book of Lazarus

AS LONG AS I don't think too much, I like my job. In the
very early morning, before you can even buy a beer to start off
the day right, you can hear a pure and willing emptiness
throughout the streets of Prague, and then it's Pavel, Janusz, and
me all making small talk on our shortwave radios as we hold
our city-issue utility signs and try to look busy. Occasionally
Pavel or I will direct traffic, but most of the time we hold the
signs and let the traffic run where it will, because, frankly, no
one follows the directions anyway. No one cares about them.
I've learned that it's best to apply my attention to the ground
beneath my feet. Is it true, I sometimes wonder, that God created the entire universe by simply uttering the twenty-two
letters of the Hebrew alphabet? If I squint my eyes, the streets
support such a theory: the split bricks and cracking stones assume the figures of kaph, nun, waw, and resh. Then I'll see
glimmers of light, shiny flashes at my feet. I'll bend over and

find a piece of gold filling gummed around stone, refashioned by the heat and the weight of vehicle tires and human feet. Thinking about tanks and riots, the terrible ways someone's dental work could have ended up stuck in the mortar, I'll feel my stomach turning. Then I'll take a better look and discover it's just gold foil, a wrapper from a piece of candy that someone has dropped.

The best days are when Janusz has drunk too much the night before and comes to work with a hangover. Then all he can manage is holding a sign, and I get the cans of paint and spray markings on the roadway, cryptic messages for the engineers, the power and water workers. The surveyors get on my nerves every now and then. They think they have something on us because their transits and theodolites cost more than our spray guns and signs. They make such a big deal out of rolling and unrolling the blueprints, adding scribbles, frowning and cursing the city architects. Still, my heart catches at the sight of those inky papers curled up in tubes. I like to think the blueprints are maps to America, a land of open borders and well-paved roads, strange rumors. Are we really to believe the grainy images we sometimes see on our TV screens, of Western road crews holding signs mounted on long poles? Do they really use headpieces in place of handheld radios, thin wires hovering next to their mouths like unfinished sentences? Thinking these things, I'll feel the blood zip through my veins. Then the surveyors will unfurl their plans and I'll see that instead of strange geographies of far-off places, they're just sections of the city in cobalt blue, laid out in fretwork that makes sense only to them or maybe to the sewer guys. Owing to all of this, I've become a professional shrugger and have learned to dismiss the banality of my job and how I do or don't do it and the insult of fate that led me away from what I wanted to do and toward what I found least despicable.

When I was eighteen, I wanted to go to university and train

for something big and vital, like law or poetry. But then the Soviet years fell upon us, and anyone with an inkling of imagination got assigned to the most mind-numbing job. Physics professors worked as window washers. Top scholars swept the trash and soot from the streets. Village idiots went into politics. University applicants from families of little standing were advised to start careers in the military, which back in 1967 seemed a good thing to do. Though it was true we Czechs had lost all seventeen wars we'd participated in over the past three hundred years—which explained our marching exercises: *Hut, two, three, I give up*—the military, for all its ills and failings, was stable. At least you knew what you were in for.

After boot camp, thanks to some incredible luck and my large frame, I was transferred to special forces, where I trained alongside the Russians, our liberators. At night, while we slept in the bunkers, we murmured strange litanies in our sleep—the parts of machine guns and their maintenance, tank defenses and formations, the proper dismantling procedures for a munitions dump—all with a loving mixture of camaraderie and slurred Russian. Lulled by the soft sounds of a language that shared so many words with our own, I told myself that the Russians could be our brothers. I believed in their utopia. But such ideology cannot suffer a change of venue or language. One summer in 1968 the Russians came down Bila Hora, White Mountain, in tanks and over bridges, into our squares.

"You sons of bitches!" my mother cried from the rooftop of our apartment building as she rained small rocks onto those former comrades, who'd engineered this swift betrayal. Together we followed the throng of people to Vaclavsky Namesti, Wenceslas Square, where protesters stuffed flowers and Czechoslovak flags down the gun barrels or took down the street signs, pointing all the one-way indicators toward Moscow and pointing the tanks back where they'd come from. Then we watched the beautiful young women in the square remove their clothes, one garment at a time, and dance in front of those tanks.

At the foot of the St. Charles Bridge, in the Old Town Square, the women seduced the drivers of the tanks, stopping them with the fluid motions of their bodies. From behind their turrets and tank portals, the Russian soldiers, most of them still boys, blushed in shame and excitement and confusion. But even the most brilliant moments fade, and it wasn't but a week later that the top brass, impervious to such charms, rolled through and we resigned ourselves to occupation. After all, it had become a well-practiced habit, a habit that suggested a tradition.

If it's true that history waltzes in a loop, then its usefulness for predicting patterns cannot be underestimated. This might explain the Czech fascination with numerology. Consider our history. In 1938 the Munich agreement was signed, a document that ceded Czech lands to Germany. In 1948 the Communist Party took control, and the great nationalist and statesman Mazyryk Jr. either jumped or was pushed from the administration building. Then in 1968 winter melted into the famous Prague Spring. The press enjoyed a brief stint of freedom: censors, with nothing to censor, whiled away their time playing checkers, and the secret police stopped wiretapping their supposed political opponents. It was socialism with a bearable, human face. But in August the Soviets invaded with their many tanks and transport planes, introducing what we now affectionately call the Period of Normalization. Even a guy like me, with my nose to the ground hunting celestial alphabets, can see the pattern.

I was thinking about this one day as I stood near Jana Palacha Square, named after the young protester and student of aesthetics who doused himself with gasoline and lit a match, setting off a string of human torches through the winter of 1969. It's hard to stand in the square without recalling those protests, especially since I was witnessing that day a scene I'd also observed nearly twenty years ago: huge gatherings of young people, students and nurses mostly, crowding the square and holding signs calling for freedom and self-determination. The difference was that on this day I held a sign too, though mine simply said YIELD, which could be interpreted as a political statement, but with my city-issue hard hat and work order, I had no reason to fear being arrested. Still, I knew how vulnerable bystanders could be here in occupied Prague, especially sign-holding bystanders, and I was a little afraid for myself, as well as for the protesters.

The air trembled with humidity, and a heavy stillness settled over the crowd. They didn't shout slogans or throw rocks. No one yelled into a microphone, and I was relieved for the steady calm, the closeness of the air that pressed us all into shifting postures. Still, I felt as if I were watching a newsreel unspool with the sound muted, and I was sure that something terrible and important was about to happen. It was, after all, the sort of moment repeated in our history. The trucks arrived with water cannons mounted over their cabs, and I thought, *This is it. They're going to blast these people right out of the square.* But at the sight of the trucks, the protesters dispersed so quietly, so quickly, I could tell they were not veteran protesters but merely students and professors and nurses on a break, hurrying through the square to get back to work.

To this day—I'm still not sure how—across the distance of the square and all those people, their placards hanging limp at their sides, the most beautiful woman in Prague spotted me. I'm not a good-looking man, and I had never been very lucky with girls. I watched with astonishment as she threaded through the crush, her back rod straight, her knees lifting into a near regulation march, walking toward me in a way that suggested resolution and defiance. *Energetic* was another word that came to mind, a word that immediately sent my bedroom imagination trotting.

She wore a nurse's uniform, sensible shoes, and a white hat stuck like a starched hankie on a mass of red hair pulled up and pinned into place. And she was small. Even with that starched cap she only reached the middle of my chest. She smiled at me, a quick smile, a flash at the mouth, and then it was gone.

"Oh," she said. "You're not Milos after all."

"No," I said.

She looked me over, took in my large, stooped frame. "Well, your back isn't straight," she said, dropping her placard on the pavement. STATE WITHOUT MALICE, the sign said.

"I'm a sloucher by nature. It's nothing serious," I said, straightening.

"Here." She took a step forward, placed one hand on my shoulder, another just below the curve of my spine. "Let me help you."

She had Ukrainian eyes, of a blue so steep they bordered on purple, and I stood there mesmerized.

"Relax," she said, pushing and pulling on me at the same time. "Better?"

I nodded and rubbed my back.

"It's Zdena, by the way," she said, holding out her hand.

I have very large hands and a great fear of accidentally hurting people with them, so I closed mine carefully around hers, which seemed as I held it in my palm too small, even for her.

"I'm Mirek," I said, bending to retrieve her sign for her. "You're very courageous."

"Ultimate freedom—political, economic, and cultural freedom—is worth dying for." Zdena pressed her mouth into a line, a challenge.

I handed over her sign. "Oh, absolutely. I couldn't agree with you more," I said, hiding my sign behind the bulk of my body. No point in bringing up my own tired recollections of boot camp and what happened to some of the courageous Czech nationals who were good fighters but bad soldiers and who realized quicker than the rest that though we had not abandoned communism, it had abandoned us long ago. Zdena gave me another one of those quicksilver smiles, and we agreed to meet for drinks after my shift. I could feel my crew boss, Janusz, eyeing us. I could almost hear him sniffing the wind like a bloodhound onto the scent of an unfamiliar idea: Mirek with a woman.

You don't plan to fall in love, you just do. Even better, love makes you stupidly, wonderfully blind, a medium-sized universal truth I was thrilled to discover. Because I loved her, I didn't care if she preferred to spend every spare moment with that underground newspaper, *Lidove Noviny,* instead of with me. I didn't care that she already had an eight-year-old son, and with him a permanent connection to Max, his father and her ex, who had a broken clock lodged in his brain that unerringly prompted him to come around for Karel when it was least convenient. The heart is large enough for anything, I reminded myself.

And I liked Karel. I liked it that with his reddish hair and violet-colored eyes, which somehow made him look like he knew things the rest of us didn't, he resembled Zdena more than Max. And there was something in Karel that reminded me of myself at his age. I imagined that over time, if I worked hard enough, we would have one of those friendships everyone talks about but no one has. I wanted to teach him to fish on the Ledhuje, maybe, or to take him to Cesky Krumlov, to the headwaters of the Vltava, tell him about spinners and lures. I wanted to tell him about the heartbreaking potential of girls. I wanted to become necessary in his life.

"I love kids," I said to Zdena on a date. Though we'd been seeing each other for about four or five months, it felt like one of those early dates that could go either way. I wasn't kidding myself. I knew part of the reason Zdena liked me was that I wasn't Max. She liked me because I didn't too often intrude in her world of the hospital. She liked me because with my green work coveralls, I had a more secure worker status under the Soviet pay structure than she did. Still. When someone likes you, a rarity for a guy like me, you easily imagine it might be love.

I'd taken Zdena and Karel to Tamaren's, a pub tucked on a side street few people find, which is how I think Tamaren preferred it. We walked to the bar, where Karel stopped to count the number of suitcases Tamaren kept by the coat rack at the door. For as long as I'd known him, it had been Tamaren's habit to bring to work suitcases stuffed full of shirts, underwear, and boxes of sugar, in case of sudden evacuation.

We found a table and Tamaren brought over a couple of pints and a Fanta for Karel, who was with great care building a tower out of beer mats.

I nodded in Karel's direction. "I love kids, I really do."

Zdena crossed and recrossed her legs, which meant either she needed to use the bathroom or she was bored already and wanted to go home. Who could blame her? She probably heard this kind of talk all the time. She probably thought, Men are dogs and they'll say anything. But could I stop talking? "Kids are wonderful," I blabbed on. "I wish I had a kid like Karel."

"Oh, Mirek!" Zdena laughed. "Maybe you should drink less. Or maybe more," she said, lighting a cigarette and blowing the smoke in my face.

On the way home, Zdena and I held hands while Karel jumped puddles along the curb. When we reached her apartment building, Karel ducked under my arm and skipped down the corridor to their flat while Zdena stayed with me at the door. Her eyes shone silver in the blue darkness, and I was a little drunk and couldn't help myself. I got sentimental.

"Marry me," I said, backing her up against the wall. I bent down to kiss her. But she smiled and dodged my lips. "OK," I said after a moment. "Then let's go inside. Together, now, and make kids like people should."

Zdena screwed up her face. "Not tonight," she said.

I shrugged, stepping back. "Move in with me, at least."

Zdena blinked. Once. Twice. Then she organized her mouth into a wary smile. "You're crazy," she said. "But OK. I'll do it."

Though Zdena assured me she was happy, she was as stingy as ever with her smiles, rationing them out only on special occasions. I'd begun to think she was a living tribute to the Czech belief that a smile gives something away, that joy on the face indicates sorrow in the soul. But then one morning I saw her in front of the mirror, pushing upward on her face with the heels of her palms, and realized that she was just afraid of wrinkles. Because Karel was in primary school already, Zdena seemed to think she was old, even though she had the face of a schoolgirl and the kind of body that would never get fat. Still, her thirtieth birthday, a time for taking inventory, was just a day away.

"Don't throw me a party," she warned.

"Too late," I said, wincing. Pavel's wife, Lujza, a woman whose voice could break rocks, had rung me a few days earlier. Talking to her had given me an instant headache behind my right eye and so, as I held the receiver out from my ear, I simply nodded and made the clucking noises of agreement. "Lujza's making a big Chinese dinner here and has already invited a bunch of girlfriends over for tomorrow night."

"That's all I need," Zdena said with a loud sigh.

The next day after work I went to get her at the hospital. I walked past the nursing station, where an orderly and a nurse fought with the plastic tubing of a plasma pack tangled around a portable IV tree. The mere sight of the pack, the color of bone marrow, made me go weak in the knees, and I decided to wait for her outside. Finally, at 6:30, Zdena appeared, her hands wet and rubbed raw from the sanitizer. I could tell from the way she uncapped a tube of bright red lipstick and ran it over her lips in one quick movement that she was upset. And now the party. I took her hand in mine and ran my thumb over the bones of her fingers.

"Don't worry so much," I said, walking her toward our flat.

"If you only knew what went on in there," she said, sighing. "Someone's been raiding the pharmacy. And then yesterday we ran out of anaesthetic in the middle of an appendectomy. Fortunately, the patient was unconscious from the pain, and later we rounded up a little extra morphine for her IV drip. After all, a person should only have to suffer so much," she said, measuring a few centimeters of air between her forefinger and thumb and giving me one of her rare smiles.

She's right, I thought. A person should only have to endure so much. And I considered myself, then, how fate owed the ugly man something, a little happiness, some beauty even. But then I wondered what I would have to pay for it in return.

When we got to our flat, Lujza threw open the door. "Finally. You're here," she said, spinning in a little circle with her arms outstretched, and I could see that she had rearranged all our furniture so everyone could fit. Pavel was in the kitchen, handing out beers, and a few of Zdena's girlfriends, women whose names I could never remember, were milling around drinking and comparing photos of their children. Pavel and Lujza's three children ran around, playing hide-and-seek with Karel, and they made so much noise that the neighbors on both sides of the flat knocked on the walls. Zdena smiled, a long tight smile that could be mistaken for a grimace of pain. She watched the children running, and I knew she was counting to ten and then twenty and then a hundred, counting her way toward calmness.

We ate kneeling at our listing three-legged coffee table, our legs tucked under and our knees sore. I had never so urgently wanted a party to end. The women next door typically clomped up and down the stairs in their block-heeled shoes, but it was nothing compared to the sound of Lujza's three children.

Lujza noticed Zdena's eyes following the children.

"You'll hear the patter of more little feet soon," Lujza said, with a touch to Zdena's elbow.

I rolled my eyes. "We're trying, dammit," I wanted to say. But why should I have to tell Lujza? I visualized myself and Zdena screwing in a mad frenzy, her friends sitting beside us, holding Olympic-style placards with numbers on them, rating us on technical and artistic merit.

After our guests finally left, Zdena started cleaning up the flat, collecting a huge mound of uneaten fortune cookies. Karel was asleep in his bed. I sat at the kitchen table, the sound of Lujza's voice still ringing in my ears. "Why do you think people like Lujza and Pavel have no problem making babies?" I asked.

Zdena blinked. She rattled some dishes at the sink. "It could be a matter of timing. It could be any number of things. After all, we're not so young," she said.

"You're thirty and I'm thirty-seven. That's not so old, either." I rubbed my forehead. "Maybe there's something wrong with me," I said at last.

"Maybe," Zdena said.

One of the advantages of the Soviet system is that when it comes to matters of medicine, the benefits are truly equitable. That is to say, whatever the ailment, real or imagined, each worker is allotted two doctor's visits per year, whether the worker needs it or not. This is why, according to Zdena, who has seen the folly of a man with a broken jaw or frayed nerves too readily using up his meager allotment of visits, it is essential to plan ahead for pain. But life's too short to salt away the days, budgeting for disaster. Which was why the next afternoon, after my shift ended, I walked to the nearest Point of Consultation Clinic. A quick phone call, some paperwork, and I found myself escorted through the corridors to Dr. Jindra's office. More than once I'd heard Zdena mention this doctor, as he was so progressive in his thinking. He even traveled to Western medical conferences and seminars, returning with satchels full of strange pharmaceuticals and apparatuses no one had ever heard of.

I waited in the outer room. "Mirek Novotny!" a nurse barked, and I followed her along a corridor thick with the smells of alcohol and sterilizer. I noted the swishing sound her stockings made as they rubbed between her thighs and against the fabric of her starched uniform. "Sit there," she said, pointing to an examining table. Then she did those things nurses always do: took my temperature and listened to my breathing, while squeezing the stuffing out my arm with that ridiculous cuff. Then *swish, swish,* she vanished into the corridor.

I sat on the table and took note of a state-of-the art treadmill stationed by the window. I remembered Zdena's remarks — how forward-thinking this Dr. Jindra was — and the mere presence of this machine launched a buoy of hope inside my chest.

Then the doorknob rattled and in came Dr. Jindra, my file open in his hands.

"Mr. Novotny." He set my file on a little table and shook my hand with vigor. "You are in excellent health. Heart and lungs good. You are not foaming at the mouth—also very good." Dr. Jindra smiled. "That was a little Slavic joke. Ha." I smiled and he shut my file. "Yes, in my student days I often wondered how to go about proving to the whole world the therapeutic benefits of laughter." He pulled on a pair of surgical gloves, and knowing what would happen next, I dropped my pants, turned my backside to him, and planted my elbows on the examining table. "At any rate, I've always said it's best to keep a light heart about this labor of love," he said. "Turn your head now and cough, please."

I looked at that treadmill and coughed. He pulled off the surgical gloves with a loud snap, and at last I could breathe again with dignity.

"You don't want to get saddled with performance anxiety on top of everything else."

I pulled up my pants and waited, I suppose, for Dr. Jindra to offer more cheer. The nurse returned and handed me a cup with a twist-top lid. She had a funny pinched look on her face, as if she was trying not to show any expression. Smiling, Dr. Jindra shifted his weight from one foot to the other. "OK, then," he said, and I realized he was waiting for me to go fill the cup.

The nurse led me to a room the size of a linen closet and held open the door for me. "Well. You know what to do," she said with a shrug, and her face slid into that expressionless look again. I realized she was not embarrassed for me; rather she was bored.

. . .

A few days later I returned to Dr. Jindra's office. The nurse, a different one from the last time, gave me an ingratiating grin that tucked in at the eyes, and I wondered if this explained why Zdena so rarely smiled—she had used them all up on the hospital patients. The nurse ushered me into Dr. Jindra's office and closed the door. Outside, in the corridor, I could hear the doctor rustling some papers. I paced around his office, hoping to find a sign of promise or an omen in his carefully arranged grouping of licenses and the framed pictures of his three perfect children.

Dr. Jindra opened the door and made his way to his desk. "Well, Mirek, your problems don't appear to be of a medical nature. Still, sometimes the parts rebel against the whole."

"So I'm not sterile?"

Dr. Jindra rubbed his neck. "Your sperm count is normal, so it could just be a matter of timing. Maybe a change in the routine, a change in diet even, might help."

"Diet?"

Dr. Jindra nodded. "One of my patients insists that when he started drinking more beer and eating less cabbage, things happened." Dr. Jindra rummaged around in his desk drawer. "So you're probably just fine, unless, of course, it's psychosomatic. Either way, you might want to give this number a ring," he said, slipping a business card into my palm. It was the number of a support group for childless men. I had never known such groups existed.

"You know, Mirek, some couples are just as happy without children, maybe even happier," Dr. Jindra said with a shrug.

I slid the card onto the edge of the desk and stood up. I did not want any more smiles or useless counsel.

The next day was one of those rainy days when each drop falls with force and ambition. Our crew was in Bubny, not far from my flat and closer still to Karel's primary school. We had to block off half the street and the sidewalk, which made a mess of traffic but gave me a good opportunity to watch all the kids, wild with joy at the sight and feel of the rain. We were cleaning up for the day, and along came Karel, his bookbag dragging behind him through the puddles, his head down.

"Karel—hey!" I waved my sign. STOP, my sign said, and Karel smiled. I dropped the sign, put my arm around him. "Let's you and me step around the corner," I said, steering him toward the opposite sidewalk.

We stood in front of a small shop. The sign said HOUSE-PLANTS, but I knew the shop also sold wallpaper, plumbing fixtures, household pets. I opened the door, and the saleswoman stationed behind a small counter looked us up and down, taking in my green coveralls, my muddy boots, Karel's bookbag.

Behind her was a long aquarium glowing green and bubbling inside. Small fish with fins as bright as birds' feathers —peacocks, even—swam in lazy circles. Through the tank I could see the stockroom and shelves of faucets and polka-dotted shower curtains. On the lowest shelves sat open cardboard boxes sprinkled with sawdust, in which I knew they kept the guinea pigs and rabbits and, on days they had them, kittens.

Karel looked through the tank to those cardboard boxes, then at me.

"We'd like to see a cat," I said to the saleswoman.

She stepped out from behind the counter. "The only ones we have now are being held for someone else. I'm sure you understand."

I glanced at Karel, who gazed down at the floor.

"But," the woman continued, "we do have a nice assortment of plastic animals." She pointed to a sad menagerie in the front window: a yellow cornsnake coiled tight, a miniature Komodo dragon far too small to inspire any sense of fear, and a huddle of shiny green turtles. Karel picked up a turtle and examined it carefully. "All right," I said to the woman, handing her some money, and we left for Tamaren's without another word.

When we got there, Pavel waved us over to a table. Tamaren followed behind, carrying a tray loaded with pints and a Fanta for Karel. "I'm thinking of applying at the plastics factory," Pavel said as soon as I sat down. "They need forklift drivers."

Karel sat two tables from us and ran his palm over the slick shell of his turtle.

"Don't do it," I said. I had heard stories of the plastics factories, of the many explosions and the expendable workers.

"It pays double what I make now plus hazard bonuses." Pavel's voice was as flat as beaten metal.

"That won't mean much when they find your arm two kilometers away. Or maybe it'll be your watch and nothing else."

"I don't care if I die from it. After all, you have to die sometime," Pavel said, reaching for his beer.

I wanted to shout, *Shut up!* with a confidence I didn't feel. Instead I shrugged and watched Karel speak tenderly to that turtle. "I don't know," I whispered. "I used to think happiness was all about procreation."

Pavel planted his elbows on the table and leaned toward me. "You can have my kids. All three of them. And I mean that."

After drinks we went home, Karel with his turtle tucked under his arm. Zdena met me in the kitchen. We had not seen each other much the last week or two—the hospital was chronically short of staff, and some of the nurses and orderlies had simply stopped going in. It occurred to me that my best hope for intimacy was to get flattened by a truck and hauled into the hospital during one of her shifts.

"I went to a doctor last week and then again yesterday," I said to her.

"You're in pain?" Zdena approached me.

"No. A man doctor, on account of a man problem. He says I should drink more beer or stop eating cabbage."

"Why?"

"So we can have a baby!" For a university graduate, she needed to have so much explained.

Zdena licked her forefinger and pressed it to the crumbs on the tabletop. "This might not be a good time for more children, Mirek. Especially since everything's so uncertain."

"What's so uncertain?" I felt my stomach lurching.

"What kind of a future would we be giving a child?" Zdena stood at the sink and turned the tap on and off. "Besides, think of all the miserable people you know—every one of them has a child. Some even have two or three. These people are miserable even if they assure everyone that they're not."

I had to resist the urge to press my palms hard into my eye sockets.

"It wouldn't be the end of the world if we didn't have a baby," Zdena continued. Now she was scrubbing the skins of carrots. "There's Karel, after all."

I put my elbows on the table and rested my face in my hands. Maybe I wanted kids for all the wrong reasons and God, who knew better, was punishing me for my incredible selfishness. Maybe I only wanted a baby so I could be like Max and have some part of Zdena that would always belong to me. Maybe I wanted a reason to relive and thus revise my own childhood. I felt movement in my stomach and the taste of bile at the back of my throat. Suddenly the floor and table were not steady enough for me and I slumped in the chair.

Zdena approached. "Let me help you, Mirek."

"No. Please. Please don't," I said, rising.

"Hold still!" Zdena pushed me back into the chair. She ground a knee into my thigh and wrenched my shoulders. I held my breath and waited for my uncooperative vertebrae to realign themselves.

"That's better now, isn't it?"

"Yes, better, I guess." I stood up and limped past Zdena, past Karel, and to the toilet, where I locked the door behind me. I unbuckled my belt, pulled down my trousers, sat on the commode, and thought about kids. I thought about Karel. A terrific kid, really, who could wipe his nose on his sleeve with the best of them. The least I could do for the boy was to get him a real turtle. Sure, the animals smelled funny, but I liked the idea of a turtle. What would it be like to have a shield so durable it could withstand anything? And turtles tended to live long, I'd heard. They could afford to be testy if they wanted to, particularly those snapping turtles that could still bite even when they were dead.

After a few minutes I heard Zdena's footsteps in the hallway. "What are you doing in there?" She knocked at the bathroom door, and I sighed, imagining my neck disappearing into a hollow cavity of chest.

I twisted toward the cabinet under the sink and fished around for some emergency toilet paper. I could feel little tubes and bottles and, way in the back, a paper sack. I pulled it out and looked inside to find a brown plastic vial. Pills, I could see that quite clearly: "*For use in case of post-procedure discomfort.*" And with the pills an instructional brochure explaining possible complications a woman might experience with the use of a diaphragm. Dr. Jindra's office phone number was stamped in bright red ink on the back of the brochure. And why not? He was, after all, very progressive.

I realized what an idiot I had been. Zdena had been dropping hints all along, but I hadn't seen them. She didn't want more children. Or, at the very least, she didn't want children with me. I wanted to bash my head against the bathroom wall and bray like the ass I was for putting myself through the humiliation of my visits to Dr. Jindra. I wanted to cry, too, for all the little people who'd been lost inside Zdena.

I stood, zipped up my pants, and washed my hands. I thought about the subtle ways in which people withdrew from their supposed loved one while maintaining the illusion that nothing was changing. I thought about the distinction between little and big truths and, more to the point, the different kinds of lies people tell. Then I thought, *This is bullshit, all this thinking,* and finally I set the brown vial in plain sight, right there on top of the toilet tank. I threw open the bathroom door and stomped through the flat to the bedroom and fell into bed, where I was determined to fall asleep and snore loudly.

After work the next day, I sat at the kitchen table with Karel as he glued together his science project—a model of a globe with interlocking tectonic pieces he'd cut out of cardboard. Zdena was due home soon, and I wondered which way it would go: a quiet and determined breakup that was swift and clean, or a bitter and loud one, with shouting and accusations and tears?

I held the pieces while Karel glued them together. I didn't want him to know that his mother and I were at odds. There is no such thing as a second childhood, though I've seen grown men tire trying to find it, and I didn't want to ruin his world of science projects and schoolboy intrigues. Still, I wanted us to continue being friends. I pointed an elbow toward his football, gathering dust in the corner. "You want to kick the ball around later?"

"No," he said without looking up. I thought I could detect a note of pity for me in his voice. "Max bought a black-and-white TV last week and I'm going to his house to watch it." Karel snapped the polar caps into place and then went into the other room, leaving his cardboard globe to weep glue onto the tabletop. I slid some newspaper underneath the dripping mess and pinched the bridge of my nose. I could feel a headache sparking behind my eyes and decided to help it along with some slivovitz I kept on top of the refrigerator. I saw the bag of fortune cookies up there too and brought the entire bag to the table and crumbled them, looking for the one fortune that would tell me how a man should live.

Just then I heard Max's tentative knocks at the door. "Come on in," I called. He opened the door carefully, as if he were afraid of what he'd find waiting behind it.

"Hey, Mirek." He took a few steps. I crumbled another fortune cookie between my fingers and pulled out a tiny slip of paper.

"*The purpose of life is to die with purpose,*" I quoted, reaching for another cookie.

"Sorry?"

"*Those who give, live,*" I read.

Max spotted Karel coming through the hallway carrying his coat. "I'm just here to pick up Karel."

"Sure. Why not," I said. "*You are a kindhearted person, mindful of others.*" This one I crumpled into a tiny ball and threw toward Max. "Want a cookie?" I asked him.

"No thanks," he said, backing through the open door and into the corridor. Karel followed without a word.

When the sun began to set, Zdena came in, clattering her keys. She held the brochure from the pills in her hand and slid it onto the table in front of me.

"So you know." She pulled a cigarette out of her purse.

I nodded. Then I laughed a strange laugh that stuck at the

back of my throat. "I really thought there was something wrong with me," I said, and pointed to my crotch.

Zdena pursed her lips and exhaled in a series of small puffs. "I'm sorry, Mirek. I really am."

I shrugged.

"I think Karel and I should leave. And"—Zdena exhaled more smoke—"that you should probably find a woman who doesn't already have all the children she wants."

I worried that I'd never again see a woman with eyes the color of Zdena's. She put her hand on my shoulder and squeezed.

"Yes." I sighed. "That's something to really think about." I didn't care anymore, was tired of caring. I put my palms over my ears.

"Don't be angry with me," Zdena said, and I could tell that already she'd forgiven herself for her small cruelties and hoped I would somehow remain optimistic about her sex in general.

"I'm not angry," I said, but even as I said it, I knew it was a lie. I slammed my fist hard on the kitchen table, and Karel's globe rolled off the edge and crashed to the floor. Zdena took a step back, and I realized that for the first time since she had known me, I had frightened her.

"I'm sorry. I'll fix it," I said, pointing to the pieces of the globe. I looked at her face, which had become impossible to decipher, and I wondered what it would take for one person really to understand another. Here she was, right in front of me, so close that I could either reach out with my hand and touch her hair or hit her. In the end, it would make no difference, because she was already gone. I looked at her purse, her oversized leather handbag that for some reason reminded me of an animal's bladder, and suddenly I just wanted her to hurry up and go.

Zdena pulled her purse strap onto her shoulder. I think she

wanted me to give her a goodbye kiss, and I wanted to be able to. It would be so easy, the easiest lie, to tell myself that this was just a date, one of those tremulous first dates when you are still learning how to read each other, and this one was just ending a little too soon. I could close my eyes, lean in, and brush my lips against her cheek. But instead I downed another shot and walked Zdena outside, my arm draped around her shoulders.

The sky seemed stuck in gray, reluctant to deepen to night. Overhead the swifts sliced through the sky with speed and grace. Though winter had passed, they were still flying south.

"Somebody better get those birds going in the right direction," I muttered, my breath singing with alcohol. Zdena shrugged off my arm.

I turned to her, surprised to see that her eyes were wet with tears. I knew well enough they weren't for me but for the situation itself. She'd return to her mother's, or perhaps move in with Max. I took a quick breath through my nose and turned my gaze to the stars that were beginning to glow.

"So. What will you do?" Zdena asked.

I shoved my hands in my pockets and turned my gaze down. I would not let disappointment and bitterness break me in two. "I think I'll get a beer," I said at last. "Then I'm going to buy a turtle."

Zdena laughed. "What are you going to do with a turtle?"

"Feed it," I said.

"Well, that's it then," she said, pulling away.

"I guess." I could feel an awakening, then, a stirring in the ground and the air. The season had turned on a hairpin, and with it Zdena. I knew already I would miss her bustling in the morning, the smell of her iron burning as she pressed her uniform. I would miss Karel and the odor of wet wool and his quiet muttering as he slowly fell asleep. I would miss the substance and warmth of their bodies and the way their sounds and their touches, as quiet and rare as they were, had transformed my ordinary life into something worthwhile.

I'm no longer looking for God in the stones of the sidewalk. I bought a turtle, and today I put dried insects in a tiny dish for him, and while I was waiting for his little head to emerge, I noticed along his shell tiny characters resembling letters of the Hebrew alphabet. Tsadhe rests above his tail, and sweeping upward in overlapping scales are mem, samekh, qoph, and taw. Some people spend their whole lives deciphering such symbols, looking for the clue that tells them who they are and how they should live, but not me. Not anymore.

When I was a boy, I had a map of the United States and Canada, which I'd lovingly folded and unfolded so many times that entire cities too close to the folds had disappeared. There's a lesson to be learned from that, I decided, carefully placing my little turtle back in his glass terrarium. It is better to imagine what is in your reach. I will stop dreaming of a place called Colorado, which is rumored to have good fishing. Instead I will make myself content with the idea of applying for a transfer, of moving to, say, Budjevice. It is, after all, the home of the Budvar beer factory. I will go there and fish in its beer-colored river. Overhead I will see the migration of birds to a new place, and in the distance the fields of mustard, which catch on fire every spring and burn brightly through summer. And inside of me I will feel that fire, that kick, the reminder that I am virile, and alive.

The Fractious South

AS A YOUNG BOY I learned many things from many wise people. It was Baba Lyuba, for instance, who told me that if a bird shits on you, it is considered extremely good luck. Before my father left for Afghanistan, he taught me that in the north a falling star was lucky, but in the south—say, in Stavropol or Nazran—it meant that a bomber had dropped for attack. From Grandpa Ilya I learned that water is life and the quiet fish swimming in it are a connection between this world and the next. And finally, from my mother, who worked in those days as a censor and translator for the Main Administration for Safeguarding State Secrets in the Press, I learned that because we were Jews, we were also invisible. This, she added, was a common enough ailment for Jews anywhere, east or west. The only people more invisible than Russian Jews, she said, were Gypsies, and Baba Lyuba explained that the Gypsies had first learned it from us.

We lived in a town just north of Rostov-on-Don, that great gateway city of the Russian south. Summers were hot. The clouds, heat-frazzled, gave up on rain and drifted emptily across the wide sky. There was never enough water to convince the dust to settle. Standing by the side of the road, I learned to read, by the shape of the dust clouds and how long they hovered, which kind of vehicle was approaching and how fast. A bicycle meant a thin ribbon of dirt shot out behind the back tire. Smaller vehicles, like a Niva or a Lada, churned up a loose swath of dirt. The Volgas, popular with the KGB, raised the road in a boxlike pattern, each shifting of the gears producing a tighter cloud in its wake. But the Kamaz and Gaz-66 transport carriers plowed the whole road up into the air, lifting the leaves of the willows and the weary aspens and coating them in distinct layers of ash-colored earth. The Gaz-66s were almost always designated as Cargo 200s, which meant they were stuffed with the bodies of dead Russian soldiers. When they passed, we all stood a little way back from the road, out of respect and in recognition of the fact that we did not want anything that had touched a Cargo 200—not even its dust—to touch us. An impossibility on our street, where Mother and Baba swept the dust from one end of the flat to the other, which was how people cleaned in summertime.

I was seven when the trouble in Afghanistan heated up. Father left town in a Kamaz headed for the Rostov military airfield. Everybody watched the convoy roll by and listened to the grumbling of the engines rattling the fine china in our cupboards.

Mother worked extra hours at the bureau, rewriting events so that the human heartache she encountered daily would sound as if it were happening to imaginary people living in far-off places. She hated that job. Truth, she confided to me one day, was a dark stain, and the words of any language were like leaves: one more way to hide ourselves from one another. The truth, she said, was that people born under the Soviet red star were doomed to move the earth with their feet, carrying their homeland from place to place. Not so long ago, she reminded

me, the Chechens had been moved from the Caucasus to Ka-
zakhstan and the Tatars from the Crimea and the Germans
from the Volga. All these people, rewriting the roads with the
soles of their feet—no wonder everyone looked so tired. "Yes,"
Mother said, as she laid her cool hand on my forehead, the
same afternoon that the sonic booms broke our plates in half,
"roads are unlucky." And I knew she was right. After all, a road
had taken my father from us.

Part of being invisible is being quiet, so if any of this bothered us, we didn't complain. Except Grandpa Ilya, who grumbled that all the dust and the noise had completely unnerved
the fish.

"They're terrified," he explained one day at the river's edge.
I was having my first fishing lesson. I leaned over the water.
Down below I could see the fish, as dark as stones, eating the
shadows of the lime trees along the bank.

"Yes, fish have feelings, just like you and me. And now they
are afraid, even when they pretend they're not." Grandpa
wiped his hands on the front of his fishing T-shirt, given to him
by a friend from the West. "Smart people aren't worth a shirt,"
it read, but he had covered the *r* in *shirt* with a piece of white
electrical tape. He could get away with such things: he had
fought the Germans in the Great Patriotic War, and he had a
piece of shrapnel in his hip to prove it. He was also famous for
having once sneaked a carp he'd poached past the police station by dressing it in baby clothes and pushing it in a little
squeaky-wheeled pram.

That summer, with a handful of worms, Grandpa and I lured
the gudgeons we liked to use for bait into biting. They were
good-looking, with their olive flanks paling to yellow and silver and then deepening again to a dark green—the kind of fish
that made me think God must have had a good time when he

painted them. But for all their good looks, God did not give them brains. It took only a few minutes to catch enough of them to start our bid for the bigger fish: pike, chub, barbel, carp, and maybe even the mythic speckled trout, a fish we talked about only in low whispers, since no one, not even the veterans who fished the river every day, had ever actually hooked one.

We fished all that summer and the following summer and the summer after that, while we awaited news of my father. And each day Grandpa Ilya taught me something new. It was Grandpa Ilya who showed me that the hook is the backbone to the bait and the connection to the fish. That with a little piece of metal, we can be made one. He didn't always know which vowels to write in some words, an *i* or a *y,* but that was all right, because he could solve difficult math problems in his head. And he had a finely calibrated sense of proportion that came from his many years of hardship and military service. In spite of all that had been done to him and all that he had done, he did not hate people; he merely hated the things they did. And it was Grandpa who told me that nothing in life could be so bad that fishing wouldn't make it better, or if not better, then bearable, or if not that, then at least fishing was a way to pass the time while waiting for your luck to change.

Over the course of the next ten years the River Don rose and fell, rose and fell, like a body breathing. In winter the water shrank and the pike floundered in the reeds and sometimes froze. In summer the water swelled. If we used balls of pork lard—which of course was completely unkosher, but necessary to hook the more discriminating fish—we might catch enough perch and carp to feed us for several weeks. Whatever the season, we began with the same rituals, me asking Grandpa if it was all right to fish at whichever spot he'd chosen and Grandpa wiggling a finger in his ear and saying, "What? What is that funny noise I hear? Such questions!" And as long as the fish had a sporting chance—that is, as long as they were in the water—any manner or method was OK. We fished, and over the course of that decade of watching the water move away from us and reshape the geography of its banks with each season, we learned to stop waiting for my father.

As time passed, Grandpa got older and a little deafer. Mother learned a few more languages and took a job with *Red Star,* the military newspaper. Baba wore filmy nightgowns over her housedress, and I married the first girl who didn't say no. I with my eyes set a little too close for anyone's comfort and Voya with her furry eyebrows and jagged teeth—we were a perfect match. We even had passion, I for the fish and she for American cosmetics, but when she was ovulating, bless her, she had some passion for me.

We just had time for a quick wedding before I was called up into the Russian Army. There was trouble in the fractious south again, this time in Chechnya, and so off went all the young men of our town: Oleg from two floors down; Good Nikolai, the kid I used to pick on, and Bad Nikolai, the kid who picked on me; and Boris, a troubled-genius type who had mapped out entire lexicons and systems of thought and had chess champion written all over him. As our sweethearts and mothers waved from the windows, we stirred up a small city of dust in our convoy of Kamazes and Gaz-66s headed to Mozdok, where we would learn the basics of bomb detonation.

When I returned home two years later, nothing was right. Grandpa Ilya spent his days sitting on a metal bench in the *dvor,* a dusty courtyard behind the apartment building. Instead of stringing his *udochki,* a fishing rod made from a birch switch, he sat tying flies he had no intention of ever using. "The fish can't even swim straight anymore," he explained.

"It's on account of those chemicals they're using in the

south," piped up Vitaly Vitaliev, the self-appointed superintendent of our building, who was famous for his mouth full of gold-capped teeth. "Ever seen a fish swim sideways?"

As if that weren't bad enough, I started hearing things. Since Oleg from two floors down had stepped on a mine and gotten himself blown to bits, everywhere I went and in everything I did I heard the sound of ticking. When I rode my bike to the river, I heard *tick, tick, tick.* Pedaling over the verge of dry grass that followed the road, *tick tick tick.* Climbing the steps to the apartment, *tick tick tick.* It haunted me, this sound.

"Idiot," Voya said on non-baby-making days.

"Stupid!" Tinke, our upstairs neighbor, tapped in code with her wrench on the water pipes. "You are hearing the sprockets from your bike."

But I knew what I heard. On this morning, as I stood on the wet bank of the river, it was Voya, resplendent with anger, her hair freshly dyed and dripping fiery orange down her neck.

"Misha!" she shouted. Her voice scattered the swifts in the lime trees, and I imagined that the fish that were waiting patiently below also scattered. Which was OK. I couldn't even hold the rod steady anymore, and I hadn't actually seen a fish in weeks: not the chubs with the metallic blue scales, or the whiskered barbels, or even the greedy pike, which liked to navigate the reeds looking for overfed and unwary ducks.

Voya perched unsteadily on the muddy bank and tried hard to look *kulturny* in her new shoes—very chic, very pointed, with mean-spirited shanks and heels. "If you can get up so early, then why can't you get a job?" Hers was a perfectly reasonable question.

I shrugged, a hapless signature move that always drove Voya nuts. I knew that she wanted evidence of some ambition for better things on my part. At the very least, she wanted me to look for work.

"Well, what do you do with yourself all day long?" She had her hands on her hips.

"Fish," I said. Before I even had time to duck, one of those prestigious shoes sliced through the air and clipped me on the back of the head. And then off she limped, *squish squish* through the mud. Every other step was murder for some unlucky worm, but a worm, unlike a man, can be broken in half and still survive.

Since I'd come back and devoted myself to a life of contemplative fishing, choosing forgetfulness as a path to healing, all Voya and I could do was fight. And drink. And fight some more. Most nights her anger burned its way through the courtyard, up the urine-scented stairs, and along the corridors of the massive concrete apartment structure. Pockmarks in the walls spoke of her many attempts to impale me with her shoes. It was a woman's way, Vitaly said, trying to console me, to express love as hatred and vice versa.

"She wouldn't keep trying to kill you if she didn't really care," he said one afternoon, his gold-plated incisors gleaming. He offered me a bottle of Crowbar. "Now drink—down to the bottom!" he commanded. I took the bottle and handed over two of the three perch I'd brought back from the river—his portion for being so well informed about so many things, like where and to whom to sell my fish, a deficit food item, and how much to ask per kilo.

It was early evening by the time we'd killed his bottle. Since they don't manufacture Crowbar bottles with resealable caps, it was our moral obligation to finish the job, Vitaly once told me. I was inclined to believe him; having been an informer for the secret police years earlier, he knew things the rest of us didn't know or didn't want to know. But Mother had explained to me long ago that Vitaly had Gypsy blood and was thus given to fanciful pranks and stories. In the main, she said, he had a bad habit of grasping at knowledge that far outstripped his comprehension. I knew Mother was right about the Gypsy part. When Vitaly heard about Oleg being blown to bits, the first thing he did was go into the courtyard. There he pressed down stones in the form of a cross until they were level with the mud, the idea being that the earth always takes back its own. Vitaly did other Gypsy things, such as cooking hedgehogs in clay. And when he couldn't find those, he cooked rats, which, frankly, are just hedgehogs that have lost their spines and thus their sense of self-worth. Vitaly liked to drink, and preferred to view life from the bottom of a vodka bottle — that was the best thing about him — and most days I even liked him, told myself that he resembled a father or an older, more calculating version of me. Thinking this way helped me overlook his completely threadbare moral development.

As evening tipped into night, the moon roiled about as if cast on fishing line. From his waistband Vitaly withdrew a second bottle of vodka. Though I already had an infant hangover threatening to cut its teeth, I kept drinking. It is, after all, considered extremely good luck to cure a hangover by pouring more booze on top of it.

"Ach, you bitch!" Vitaly shouted. Though he held the bottle at arm's length, I knew the gesture signaled his deep affection. "Speaking of dogs," he said, pointing to an old edition of *Izvestiya* scattered at the bottom of the stairs, "those Chechens — who do they think they are? Savages — they deserve what's coming to them!"

I winced and wagged my head from side to side. I'd seen a lot of bad things happen to people I knew, people just like us. Oleg, of course, was irretrievable. And Boris, the troubled genius, whose dark hair had turned chalk white in the course of a single maneuver. If his army-issue assault weapon had spilled innocent blood, then why not guilty blood? he asked. And the next day, with a coat hanger rigged to the trigger, he shot himself. Good Nikolai and Bad Nikolai: both of them dead. Their bodies torched, their eyes open to see it. Yes, bad things happen. And nobody knows it better than those of us who came home.

"You should go back and kick their asses, boyo." Vitaly gave me the bottle. "You should do it for Mother Russia."

"It's something to think about," I said.

Vitaly smiled, and a gold tooth winked. He rubbed his hand on my head, the Gypsy reminder to stop thinking.

By the time we finished the bottle, light had seeped over the hills, turning the clouds the texture of curdled milk. The hammers inside my head had quieted to a bearable rhythm, but I could hear Baba Lyuba and Tinke arguing again. I trudged past Vitaly and up the stairs to the third-story landing. Mother was scurrying around, darting into the open apartment, then rushing out again. First looking for her coat. Then for her hat.

"What is going on?" Grandfather Ilya's voice followed her.

"Nothing important," Mother said, rushing back in for her purse.

"What, then?" came Baba Lyuba's voice.

On the landing Mother brushed a kiss on each of my cheeks, then tipped her chin toward Baba. "Yeltsin is having trouble with his heart again," she said, and disappeared down the stairs. Before the outer door had even fallen back into the locks, Baba was wailing. And me thinking the whole time she'd gone barking mad. Who could weep for a man like that? But then, as the bent rims of worry went around and around, I realized that Mother had been speaking in military euphemisms again. Yeltsin's heart trouble meant another major operation in Chechnya, and she had to make it sound good before the next day's papers hit the stands.

· · ·

"*Mi*-sha!" Voya's alto voice broke in half, summoning in an instant the hangover hammers. Then she appeared on the landing. She glared at me and brushed a brittle strand of hair behind an ear. She'd dyed it again, this time the color of cadmium rage. "I can't live like this forever," she said.

"How else should we live?" I asked, ducking through the open door of the apartment.

"Better. We should live better and we should have things."

"What things?"

"Things. An apartment to ourselves." Voya waved her thermometer at me. "Babies."

Such impossible desires, especially since we had all the typical post-Soviet problems—we were in possession of some brains and absolutely no clout or money. In the same boat were my mother and Grandfather Ilya and Baba Lyuba. Which was why we all lived together in the first place, our sleeping areas cordoned off with a complicated network of towels hung as curtains from clotheslines.

"Don't *you* want things?" The bottom dropped out of Voya's voice.

Baba Lyuba looked at me, clicked her tongue in disappointment, and turned back to the TV, winking and blinking there on the reinforced cardboard box it came in.

On the screen was an old broadcast of Yeltsin addressing a crowd. Even though he had a way of thrusting out his neck in order to lose his double chin and make his jaw stronger, he didn't look good on camera. There were big problems in the south, Yeltsin said, but all I heard was the old Soviet slogan: "With an iron hand we will drive humanity to happiness!" Yeltsin raised a fist, and the people, hearing strong words that suggested purpose, words we all like to hear sometimes, clapped and shouted. In the corner of the screen a clock kept time, the second hand ticking loudly, as if to remind us all to keep breathing.

"Do you hear that?" I turned to Voja.

"What?" She sniffed the air.

"What?" Grandpa Ilya shouted.

Then with her wrench Tinke from upstairs tapped out in code, *What? What?*

"That ticking!" I cried.

Responding to some ancient cue, Baba Lyuba jumped up and ran around the room opening and shutting doors and peering into the cuffs of sleeves, both her own and those belonging to others. Old habits die hard, and Baba was, if anything, a creature of habit. But she could assemble a Kalashnikov in less than fifteen seconds, so if she wanted to wear flimsy lingerie and shout, I say do what makes the most noise and be happy.

Then from behind our layer of privacy towels came Voya's voice, strangely modulated to something like tenderness. "*Misha!* Come here!"

I stepped behind the towel curtain. Voya slid her nylons to her shins, and I studied her thighs and the sliver of light that shone between them. She waved the thermometer at me. Ah. A baby-making moment.

Good taste and good sense impose certain limits, but never in my life have I been accused of possessing either. And it's hard to say no to Voya. Off came the pants. Then, in labored silence, Voya and I set about doing what a man and a woman must do. Baba coughed and dragged the kettle over the ring, doing everything she could to convince herself that she wasn't hearing what she full well knew she was hearing, while Tinke kept clanking at the pipes. Add to this the noise of Vitaly playing sentimental songs on a paper and comb, exploring the metaphysical riffs and eddies of this life as clarified by the vapor fumes of his rapidly emptying vodka bottle: "Which proves that creation began on a Tuesday, which is all the more reason to drink on a Monday." Vitaly's wisdom drifted up through our open window. Through all of this I could sense Grandfather Ilya in his chair, looking at his Western fly-tying manual, recalling, I suppose, all the fish that had gotten away.

When the baby-making rendezvous was over, Voya rolled out from under me and took her temperature again. A golden moment, because it is nearly impossible to utter demeaning observations with a thermometer in your mouth. But then out came the thermometer, and it was all systems go.

"This business in Chechnya. Vitaly says it'll be over before it even really starts."

"I don't know." I shook my head, remembering what I'd seen through the tank portals. "The Chechens can knock out tanks as well as anybody else."

"Lots of guys are going anyway. It's a job. It's good money."

"Maybe." I shrugged. "I don't know."

"You don't know much, do you?" Voya said, more amazed now than angry.

I thought of Boris and dropped my head to my hands. "Sometimes it's better to be a happy idiot," I said, groaning.

"Well, good news. You're halfway there." Voya pulled on her nylons. "I suppose you'll go fishing now."

Mention an itch and a scratch is sure to follow. I grabbed my net and rod and flew down the stairs.

Vitaly met me at the bottom. He had another issue of *Izvestiya* in his hand, the paper rolled up tight. "Boyo." He draped an arm over my shoulder. "I like you. You're not too bright, but you try hard. That's why I'm telling you something I haven't told any of the other guys."

"What?"

Vitaly laid a finger alongside his nose. "Things."

"What things?" At the open window above us, Baba's head appeared between pots sprouting little yellow stars, the flowers of future tomatoes.

"Things," Vitaly said, wheeling me closer to the building. "For instance, if you were to go back and participate in a military operation, you'd receive five million rubles."

"Five million!" I heard Baba yell up to Tinke.

"If the operation were successful, three million more. For knocking out a tank or an armored vehicle, an additional three million. The destruction of a self-propelled artillery gun would get five million." Vitaly stopped to catch his breath.

From our window I could hear Voya on the phone with a girlfriend: "Does it have a real oven—the kind you bake things in?" Her voice cartwheeled up the octaves. Yes, she wanted things.

Then Mother came through the *dvor,* back already from the bureau, in her hands the latest edition of *Red Star.*

"What happens if I die?" I whispered.

Vitaly could hardly contain himself. "Then your family would be paid a hundred and thirty million rubles. Think of it! Brilliant, and so simple. Only a real idiot could screw this up."

"But I was only a foot soldier."

"Pah." Vitaly waved a hand at a mosquito. "I can fix it so that you were and still are elite Kantemirov, Fourth Tank Division."

But Mother, who knew more about it than Vitaly ever could, shook her head sadly. "Don't listen to him," she said, so quietly it could have been another mosquito buzzing at my ear.

Vitaly stuffed his hands in his pockets and considered the possibilities. "Yes, I can fix it. For half your pay, I'll fix it. It's so simple, really."

I looked at my rod and net. I thought of the logic of water. How it is necessary sometimes for one creature to trade its life for another. The worm for the chop, the caddis for the trout.

"Do it for God," Vitaly said. "Or do it for your family," he added gently. Then he lifted his gaze to Grandfather Ilya, wedged next to Baba and peering down at us from beside the tomato pots. "Do it for all those Chechen fish. In the mountain lakes, they have trout the size of big dogs."

Down the street a convoy of Gaz-66s moaned. The spell broken, Mother moved past me, her head down.

Yes, the Chechen trout are legendary. In the high lakes of the Sunzha region lives the pacha-chaar, the kingfish. Mother told me that when Czar Alexander II first ate this trout, he developed such a taste for it that he immediately had some sent by rail to St. Petersburg in cars equipped with oversized aquariums. Ever since, anglers have been relentless in the pursuit of the pacha-chaar, that trout with the golden scales and regal mouth. Violet at the gills and spotted in places, it is like a finned leopard. And exceedingly wise. This fish knows the number of days a man has left to live, and if you hook it, it must tell you your fate.

I counted the steps up to the landing. Mother was waiting outside our apartment. She kept her head down and the newspaper clutched to her chest. But over the top of her glasses, she fixed her eyes on mine. "He's dangerous, you know. His ideas are like his vodka—cheap and intoxicating," she said, pushing open the door.

Later, at the cardboard table, Mother spread out an old edition of *Red Star* while Baba and Voya poured tea and set down white bread and a small bowl of dark cherries. We all ate and drank in silence. Grandfather Ilya finished tying a dark Cahill fly, the ginger hackles fluttering seductively with every movement of the air. Voya checked her reflection in the belly of the silver coffeepot, so tarnished by time it had a purple sheen like a pike's flanks. Her eyebrows had thinned a bit, and I knew that despite her rage, she really was worried.

Baba spilled some tea on the newspaper and leaned to examine the damage. The red star had smeared, the ink staining the table underneath. "Oh, if only you-know-who were still alive," she said, touching the wet star. "Yes, things would be better. He was a true hero."

Mother jumped from her chair, her hand raised as if she were going to strike Baba. "How can you say that after what he did to Jews!"

Baba leveled her gaze at Mother. "Stalin won the war. And there was bread in the shops. Every day." She poked at the bread on her plate. "And I don't mean this stuff here."

Grandpa pinched the Cahill fly between his forefinger and thumb and held it up. "Listen to us!" he said to the fly. "If God is home and goodness the land we are searching for, then we are in a far country," he said, dropping the fly.

"Yes," Baba said, hanging her head. "But it is still our country."

Mother carried her teacup to the sink, the cup trembling in the saucer. Voya popped the last cherry into her mouth, hooked an arm through mine, and led me to our sanctuary behind the towels.

"Your grandmother!" she rolled the cherry from one side of her mouth to the other.

I shook my head. "The thing to remember about Baba is that she honestly thinks the dead come back to see who's wearing their shoes and to reclaim beloved handbags."

"Still, she has a point. War is good business. Especially if you win." The stone of the cherry knocked between Voya's teeth.

"Yes, but these Chechens—they are people just like us. If they want their own patch of dirt, some rocks, why not let them have it?"

"So stay if you want. I don't care!" Voya said at last, spitting out the stone. It flew through the air and stuck to my shirt. "Just do something besides fish!"

I reached for her shoulder, and she sank to the mattress and began to weep, her sobbing grand and troubled and mysterious all at the same time. I held her—or rather, she allowed me to hold her—and eventually she wiped her nose on my shirt.

"Oh, Misha, you are like a child," she said, her chin wobbling. "I can't be angry with a child." She stuck her thermometer into her mouth and I counted the seconds. Then she yanked the instrument out and frowned. "No," she said, waving the thermometer in the air. "And not right here, either." Then she pulled the bed sheet up over her head and fell fast asleep. Just like that.

They say we dream at night of what we want by day but don't have the words for. In the daytime we are poor, our words flimsy, but nighttime makes us rich, the images of the big and small things we desire swirling about as if they were ours already. As I slept, pictures trotted across my eyelids and I dreamed of Voya besieged by an army of toasters. I saw Baba Lyuba and fourth-story Tinke, reconciled at last, floating downriver in Tinke's washtub while Baba navigated with her mop. For Grandpa Ilya, I dreamed of a complicated three-tiered tackle box complete with chenille, peacock burls, long ringneck rooster hurls, lead wire, and the lemon-colored side feathers of a duck—everything he would need to make flies that would fool even the most discerning fish. For Mother, who only wanted to live on the bread of faithful speech, I dreamed of newspapers with blank pages.

For myself, I dreamed of the silent wrasse, with a bolt of iridescent silver scales and mandarin orange flames running along its flanks. I dreamed of weed beds full of pike and reeds full of perch, the black-tailed dace and the mythic taimen of the Siberian rivers, and all the fish quietly sleeping on the other side of the world.

A dog barked. Voya stirred and muttered, "Idiot!" Even in sleep she was angry, her eyebrows stitched together. I pulled on my boots, crept through the flat and down the corridor, and tiptoed past Vitaly, asleep in the stairwell.

The air was heavy, splitting at the seams. It was one of those foggy, melting mornings, good for tossing coins and not looking where they fall. I got on my bike and headed for the river and imagined, as I pedaled and the bike squeaked and ticked, that it was singing sad songs, saying with its squeaks and groans all that I wished I could say and knew I never would.

When I reached the river, the veterans had already stretched their nets over the best spots. Upriver, the young boys, on summer holiday and bored, acted out the Book of Revelation. They threw rocks at each other, mimicked the various plagues described in that terrible book. Two boys tortured a hapless frog. Two others pretended the river had turned to blood. And because I had a patchy beard and close-set eyes, they called me Jesus. As I pedaled by one of them, a stone whizzed past my ear.

"You're dead!" the boy shrieked. I stopped my bike and turned to him. It was Oleg's little brother, Yuri. "I lobbed a grenade at you and you're dead!" Yuri jabbed the air between us with a stick. I started pedaling again, and my bike went on ticking, all the way downriver to the place where the rocks broke the current. The water smelled like metal and the air smelled like earth. I planted my feet in the dirt, my body hollow and aching but my hand steadier than it had been in months. Then I cast, my line cutting into the water like a razor.

I stood like that for hours, watching the sun slide through the sky. I was thinking about the fish, how they live their whole lives fighting water. They charge against the current, pushing for spawning waters. It's almost a shame to hook them and pull them in, bucking and chuffing the whole way. And then I felt a tug. I tightened my grip on the pole and hauled in the line. A speckled trout! How it had escaped the nets of the veterans, I couldn't even guess.

We fought for a while, me hauling the line, the fish trying to slough off the hook. At last I worked the trout to the shallows. But as I lifted it from the water and onto solid ground, it whipped its body around, thrashing against the hard-packed earth, croaking and whistling, angry to have been landed. Some people may not think much of the speckled trout, but when it was on the bank gasping and fighting for air, the light caught its orange fins and red flanks, and I saw for myself how beautiful a fish it was. I wanted to touch its heaving sides, make sure its scales weren't in fact gutter-shot gold. So pure and brave a fish, I was almost sorry to see it come to this.

Then I stabbed it and cleaned it quickly. I killed it because that's what I had been taught to do, and I was taught we were not bad people for doing this. I thought of Good Nikolai, Bad Nikolai, of Boris. After all, even the beautiful and strong sometimes pay with their lives. And where I had only moments earlier stood in amazement at this beautiful fish, its strong body and its powerful fins that had once suggested flight, I was now saddened to have been the reason for its demise.

I bent and washed my hands in the river. Then I stepped out of the water, slid the trout inside my shirt, felt its slick skin against mine, and pedaled away. The whole way home I felt as if I had swallowed a sharp river reed that had lodged inside my chest. When I opened my mouth for air, a hollow sound came whistling out of my throat. And inside my head, that old ticking, marking tick by tick the retreat of the clouds and their slow cooling from the colors of fire to dusk: pink to purple, to the same hue of a bluing plate along a rifle, and then to ash. By the time I made it to the *dvor,* the moon was tethered to the hills, a full, concrete moon, the kind that turns men into animals, causes dogs to bark and married couples to fight.

When Vitaly saw me, he peeled himself from the stone archway. A cloud of mosquitoes followed him, a buzzing halo about his head and ears. He stopped, brought a flask to his mouth. I stood, mesmerized, watching the bobbing of his Adam's apple. Up, down. Up, down.

"Good news, boyo! I've arranged everything!" he shouted once he'd finished drinking. As he approached, the mosquitoes wobbled away, dizzy. Somehow Vitaly looked longer of tooth. From his pocket he withdrew a shot glass. A real drinking glass! He handed me his flask. I could smell the watered-down rocket fuel inside. "Pour!" he ordered, and it struck me again, as I carefully rimmed the glass, how amazingly wolflike Vitaly had become in the light of this concrete moon.

"So. You're going. Next week. Drink!"

I drank.

"Yes, you'll go and have a wonderful time. Go down there and show them who's boss. You'll feel a thousand times better. And finally you'll get the respect you deserve."

"No." I shook my head. "I don't think so."

From the fourth-floor window, Tinke's head emerged, and at our window were Baba and Voya, their hair dyed in companion shades of purple.

"Yes, you'll go and be a thousand times richer," Vitaly said.

I thought of the fish in my shirt, of all the fish I wanted to catch, how along their scales entire decades can flit from shimmer to shadow. "No. I'm not going."

Vitaly blinked, as if in the presence of an unexpected joke. Then he smashed his glass against the stone bench. "You coward! You dirty coward!" he bellowed, his fury absolute. Then he lowered his head and charged. He hit me, hard, in the stomach, and I fell against the stairs. My beautiful speckled trout slipped to the ground.

I looked at the fallen fish and felt within me such a mixture of rage and sorrow and lunacy that I almost understood why men kill each other. I reached for my trout, and Vitaly lunged again. At that moment a tomato pot whizzed from high above and clipped him on the shoulder. He staggered and collapsed against the bench. It was a long and thick silence that lay there between us. And then Vitaly grinned.

"Now *that's* true love," he said, fanning the air about his face with one hand and pointing to our tomato pot with the other. I looked at the plant, the scattered dirt, the shards of the pot. Somewhere underneath all the mess was my speckled trout, pulverized.

Vitaly took a liberal drink from his flask, then pointed his nose toward the moon and howled.

I trudged up the stairs to our apartment. Voya met me at the door, took my hand, and led me to our sagging mattress. We sat in silence, listening to Vitaly and to the sounds coming from the road: even at this late hour the Kamaz trucks rattled and whined as they headed for Mozdok. I thought of how history repeats itself in such sounds, in the growls of tanks and the booms of supersonic jets. How in this way entire centuries are recalled in the return of the same weary dust.

I looked at Voya. Her violet hair hung in her face. "Who were you aiming for—me or Vitaly?" I asked her.

She ran her hands over her dress, smoothing the fabric with her fingers.

"You're right," I said. "It doesn't really matter."

"Tell me things will change," she said. Her voice sounded irremediably sad. It was as if she had swallowed the same reed I had, and it changed the texture of her words from anger to a great and jagged sorrow. Through the veil of her hair I could see her mascara running.

"Things will change," I said, but I could hear how empty my words sounded against the rumblings of the convoy outside the window. And then there was Vitaly, howling at the moon. Baba drifted to and from the windows, conferring with Tinke.

"Well," Tinke called, "he always was an exhibitionist."

"He'll probably take off his shirt," Baba said.

"Or worse, recite a poem," Grandpa Ilya shouted.

Mother laughed, and it was such a sweet sound, like water, I thought that in all this madness, such a sound might save us.

"Come closer," Voya said, unbuttoning my shirt. The concrete moon threw a wash of silver over our mattress. Voya kicked her stockpile of shoes into the corner and pulled her dress over her head. The light of the moon illuminated her neck and shoulders and her very *kulturny* Western brassiere. Ah, the concrete moon! It was, after all, the kind of moon that made crows fly backward and wheat grass volunteer beside the road. A moon that asked the dust to settle, winked at stolen kisses, and caused the early stars to bloom in the sky and tomatoes to ripen on the vine. Voya kissed me then. Such kisses! With the first kiss I was transported to the days before I knew what a war was. With the second kiss I was returned to the red passion of our youth, and with the third to renewal, to being brought back from the dead, remade from mud.

ACKNOWLEDGMENTS

Endless gratitude to Julie Barer, who brought this book into the world, and to Heidi Pitlor, whose keen eye and guidance made the stories sing.

Grateful thanks to the Ruth Hardman family, to Jeffrey and Mary Hindman of the Hindman Foundation, to the entire Nimrod staff and especially Francine Ringold, to Clem Cairns and Jula Walters of Fish Publishing, and to the Oregon Arts Commission, Oregon Literary Arts, Inc., and the Money for Women/Bobby Deming Memorial Foundation for awards that supported the writing of these stories.

Gracious thanks to the Humanities Department at George Fox University, the English Department at Iowa State University, and the Creative Writing Department at University of Oregon. I am grateful for the generous and wise instruction of Becky Ankeny, Carol Edgarian, Barbara Haas, Ed Higgins, Ehud Havazelet, Tom Jenks, Robert Olmstead, Steve Pett, Rebecca Stowe, and Ray A. Young Bear.

I am profoundly indebted to my friends for their encouragement, support, and wisdom in the crafting and revision of these stories: Don Comfort, Willing Davidson, Liz Duvall, Teresa Heesacker, Ben and Colleen Jeffery, Raffi Khatchadourian

Dave Mehler, Bernie Meyer, Tania Morris, Jane Poole, Chris and Rebecca Skaggs, and Geronimo Tagatac.

"The Fractious South" is dedicated to the Coffee Cottage Luftmenschen. "A Darkness Held" is for Bernie Meyer. "The Hurler" is for Brian. "Halves of a Whole" is for Colleen McDonough.

Thanks to my father, Richard Withnell, for his enduring support and patience. Thanks to my mother, Gayle Withnell, who gave me her love for language. Thanks to Ken and Danya Ochsner for tolerating the artistic temperament and caring so wonderfully for their grandchildren. Thanks to Dave, Lora, Dan, and Jake Withnell, the entire Cade and Endres clan: Chrisse, Chuck, Justin, Erica, Vanessa, and Katrina, Marge, Steve, Billy, Jane, and Judy. My thanks to Jill and Bader Mahnane, Jenni Ochsner, Jenny and Joe Potmesil, Andrea and Alex Moore, Aaron and Lisa Harris, Mike and Dolores Harris, Ginger Stratton, Julea and Jeff Twedt, Lissa and Sean Smith, Lynn Meiseger, Laurie DeHosse, Mike and Monica Rohrer, Dale and Phyllis Sylvester, Ferd and Gerry Ochsner. Some of you fed and cared for me. All of you patiently listened and quietly believed in me.

My thanks to Judy and Dave Barker, Dace Berzins, Sally Brinker, LaShaun Gray Chapman, Maureen Clifford, Andrea Cornachio, Serena Crawford, Matt Crutchley, Shannon Dobson, Jennifer Harris, Adrianne Harun, Suzanne Heath, Cory Holding, Sheree Jensen, Philip Montoro, Paige Newman, Matthew Perez, Rolf Potts, Catherine Segurson, Clem Starck, Ana Stoparic, Dusti Wallace, and Estera Wieja for their ce in my life.